## About the Author

MAGGIE CONWAY lived the first ten years of life in London before moving to Scotland. She has a degree in English Literature and spent many years working in offices dreaming of pursuing her passion for writing.

A perfect day would include an early morning swim, a good coffee, a great book and a few hours spent writing before the chaos of a husband, three children, a dog and a cat begins.

Having landed the role of chief dog walker, she spends far too much time roaming the streets but at least this gives her a chance to think up new storylines.

## Also by Maggie Conway

*Winter at West Sands Guest House*

# Summer at West Sands Guest House

## MAGGIE CONWAY

ONE PLACE. MANY STORIES

HQ
An imprint of HarperCollins*Publishers* Ltd
1 London Bridge Street
London SE1 9GF

This paperback edition 2018

1

First published in Great Britain by
HQ, an imprint of HarperCollins*Publishers* Ltd 2018

Copyright © Maggie Conway 2018

Maggie Conway asserts the moral right to be
identified as the author of this work.
A catalogue record for this book is
available from the British Library.

ISBN: 9780008320447

MIX
Paper from
responsible sources
FSC™ C007454

This book is produced from independently certified FSC™ paper
to ensure responsible forest management.

For more information visit: www.harpercollins.co.uk/green

Typeset by Palimpsest Book Production Ltd, Falkirk, Stirlingshire
Printed and bound in Great Britain by
CPI Group (UK) Ltd, Melksham, SN12 6TR

# Chapter One

Molly Adams peered into the bottom of the laundry basket. The few items of clothing barely warranted a whole wash cycle but she reached down and bundled them into the machine anyway. She didn't want anything lying about tomorrow, least of all her dirty washing.

A surprising array of internet recipes and supermarket meals for one had taken care of her eating but laundry for one had taken her by surprise, an unexpected consequence of her husband leaving her.

Standing in the small utility room, she let out a sigh. With its integrated appliances and fitted shelves, she'd always quite liked the warmth and cocoon-like feel of the small space and she stood for a few moments almost reluctant to move. The silence of the house was driving her mad and even the gurgling and slurping of the washing machine was welcome.

Funny, it had been the laundry basket – or at least its contents – that had first alerted her. She could still recall the moment her insides had shifted uneasily as the unfamiliar scent wafting from her husband's shirt assaulted her senses. She had placed the shirt in the washing machine, setting the dial to the highest temperature – totally unsuitable for the luxury two-ply fabric Colin favoured. Part of her had hoped the shirt might disintegrate in the wash. Perhaps if she destroyed the evidence, they could carry on as normal. Except deep down, she had known normal wasn't good. She had noticed a brightness in her husband's eyes, a spring in his step that she knew wasn't of her making.

She hadn't confronted him immediately, hadn't been in a particular hurry to have the conversation that might end their five-year marriage. Because although she had wondered about the state of their marriage for some time, she certainly hadn't expected her husband's infidelity to bring it to an ignominious end. She needed to live with the notion that her husband was having an affair, to bolster herself for what she knew was surely to come. She thought she should be rallying herself to put up a fight to save their marriage, except she wasn't sure exactly what she would be fighting for.

She had tried to pinpoint the moment their lives seemed to have veered in different directions. Molly had known Colin was driven but it wasn't until after they were married that she realised just how ambitious he really was. It seemed with every step he took up the corporate ladder he also took a step further away from her.

Molly supposed she'd always been more of a dreamer, not just in her career but in life generally. She liked to view the future as an unknown quantity, new things to discover, surprises still to come. Colin on the other hand was a planner and liked to look ahead – preferably with a spreadsheet involved. She began to feel caught in his tailwind, always trying to keep up with him.

A year ago, Molly had been made redundant at the same time Colin had gained a big promotion in the financial company where he worked. She was proud of his success and he was sympathetic for her loss but instead of pulling them closer, it had the opposite effect. While his career soared, Molly's had stalled and she'd taken a temporary position covering maternity leave. Colin clearly wasn't impressed with her temping status; Molly suspected it annoyed him that she wasn't following a clear career path.

At school Molly had been undecided about her future, shuf-
fling along to the careers teacher admitting she didn't have a clue
what she wanted to do. Somehow between them, they'd conjured
up marketing and so after school she started her degree.

In her first year at university, Molly had met Declan, an effortlessly cool and impossibly good-looking arts student from Galway
who told Molly her wild red hair and emerald green eyes reminded
him of home. Her hair was closer to brown than red and her
eyes were hazel but who was she to argue with such romanticism?
Until then, her only experience had been clumsy, fumbling
encounters with boys she knew from school. She had never met
anyone like him and she was soon spending every minute she
could with him – all her good intentions of working hard flying
out the window. When, after several months, the relationship
ended as suddenly as it had started, the resultant fallout had been
responsible not only for breaking Molly's heart but also for her
failing all her exams.

Studying for her resits during a miserable summer Molly
wondered if university was right for her. But she had buckled
down, passed all her resits and started second year determined
to do well. From that point on, when she wasn't attending lectures
she squirrelled herself away in the library. It was there one day,
when she was stretching for a book on the top shelf, that a safe
pair of hands had reached out and prevented it from toppling
on her.

She had turned to find Colin. Handsome and serious, Molly
had immediately fallen for him, impressed by his focus and self-
assuredness. She liked that he was organised and remembered
important dates. What he may have lacked in spontaneity (Declan
had once turned up with a picnic and whisked her away from
classes to spend the day at Loch Lomond), he made up for in
dependability (she recalled all the times Declan had never showed
up).

Studying economics, Colin was two years ahead of Molly so

that by the time she graduated, he was already on his career path. On the day of her graduation Molly had been surprised but delighted when Colin offered her a dazzling engagement ring which she had readily accepted. She knew they were young but she had seen that as a good thing, a sign they were meant to be together.

Using her parents' perfect marriage as her guiding light, Molly knew she had found the right man to follow in their footsteps. She had been full of hope on the day of her wedding; this was the start of her fairy tale and she had no reason to suppose it wouldn't last.

But then came the day of the laundry discovery. When several days had passed and Molly finally gathered her courage to talk to Colin, he'd admitted to the affair immediately and told her he was leaving. She couldn't believe that he hadn't wanted to discuss it, that he was so ready to throw it all away.

'Aren't we at least going to talk about it?' she'd asked him.

'It's too late, I'm sorry.' He'd shuffled on his feet awkwardly, unable to meet her eye. Beneath his contrite expression, Molly saw relief and she knew there was no way back for them. She looked at him, wondering what had happened to the man she had married.

Gone was the man she'd trusted and thought she'd grow old with. In his place there was a man she barely recognised. One who had become very particular about the clothes he wore and the car he drove, and preferred dinner parties to nights in the pub. One who spent more time at work than at home and took business calls before hers. One who had lied and cheated.

A woman at work was enough information for Molly. She resisted asking for the details – what good could come from knowing when it had started, if he'd bought her gifts, if they'd shared a hotel room at the conference he'd attended in Paris. No, she refused to acknowledge the cliché their marriage had become.

Colin moved out quickly, clearly in a hurry to get on with his new life. Strange, difficult days followed. At times Molly felt like running away – where to, she had no idea. But running wasn't an option; she had her job to go to and didn't want to let anyone down. And it had been the job that had acted as a life-raft of sorts, giving her a routine and a reason to get out of bed each day.

So Molly had remained in the house on her own, desperately trying to cling to normality. Functioning on automatic pilot, she went to work and avoided people. She'd told only those who needed to know, which turned out to be not many. Cossetted in what she thought was the security of her life with Colin, letting friendships fade had been all too easy. Colin told her to keep the house as if he were doing her a massive favour but the truth was, she'd never really liked the house.

It had been Colin who insisted they go and see a new-build estate on the outskirts of Glasgow. Molly's dream of starting married life in a spacious red sandstone in the West End, of weekends spent painting, varnishing floorboards and strolling around the bustling bars and vintage shops were slowly extinguished by the gushing sales advisor fawning over the flawless finishes of the contemporary kitchen and the dual-aspect bay-windowed lounge.

She'd turned to Colin, his eyes shining.

'There's not much character,' she'd whispered to him.

'Who cares about character? With the deal they're offering first time buyers we'll be quids in, we won't do any better than this.' With little or no knowledge on such things she had bowed to his financial acumen. She'd simply been happy there were four bedrooms and had felt a little inner glow as she imagined children filling the rooms.

She had tried to make the most of the house but no amount of coloured cushions, clever lighting or potted plants ever seemed to infuse any real warmth into it. It had always felt soulless to her. The first few times Molly had driven into the cul-de-sac of identikit houses, she struggled to recognise her own home and had resorted to placing a bright yellow plant pot outside their front door.

All their neighbours appeared happy enough with families coming and going. Some mornings Molly would see a group of women clad in tight black Lycra, meeting after the school drop to go for a power walk. Other days they morphed into sleek looking businesswomen, suited and booted, jangling keys and driving off in their Mercedes or BMWs. She thought maybe she'd join their ranks one day but anytime she raised the subject of children, Colin managed to sidestep the issue. Now she was certain he'd never had any intention of starting a family and the thought made her stomach knot in anger.

Wandering through to the front room, Molly wasn't sure how she had got through the last few months. She'd rattled about the house on her own, trying to find comfort in being able to leave clutter lying around, cry at romantic films and read until midnight with the light on, her once endearing habits that had clearly come to annoy Colin.

Colin hadn't wanted to take much and there was little evidence that he'd ever lived here. She almost marvelled at how efficiently he had extracted himself from her life. He handled the dissolution of their marriage the way he handled everything, and she was subjected to his ruthless efficiency for one last time. She certainly didn't want to prolong it or demean the situation further by haggling or stalling for time but all the same was shocked by just how quickly and clinically Colin was treating their divorce.

Apparently, if neither of them contested their 'irretrievable breakdown', it could all be over in weeks. With no children involved, all they had to do was agree over property and financial matters. He'd done all the paperwork and she just needed to sign on the dotted line. All so simple.

When Colin had brought round the papers for signing, Molly had inadvertently seen The Other Woman pacing up and down at the side of Colin's car, taking a phone call. She had to admit, she didn't look a total lush. Ultra slim with a sleek bob and a dark business suit, Molly couldn't help thinking she'd been traded in for a more efficient model. Because although Molly hadn't grilled Colin for details, that hadn't stopped her imagining who the other woman was, how much more beautiful and talented she must be. In some ways, that she looked so normal made her feel worse; it was easier to think of her as some evil temptress intent on wrecking their marriage.

Molly also discovered that day why Colin wasn't overly concerned about the house and its contents. Not even trying to conceal his excitement, he told Molly he was relocating to the company's head office in New York – presumably with *her*. When he told Molly it was a dream come true, she had swallowed with difficulty. It was a dream he had never shared with her.

In the kitchen now, Molly glanced at the oversized retro clock hanging on the wall, willing time to speed up. Now that she was going, she wanted to get on with it. More for something to do than a desire for caffeine, she decided to make herself a coffee. She'd never got the hang of the fancy coffee maker Colin had insisted on buying despite its astronomical price. Still, it had outlived her marriage, she thought savagely as she watched the thick black liquid trickle into a cup.

Carrying it through to the hall Molly studied her reflection in the hall mirror.

On the surface, she looked more or less the same. Her auburn hair was longer than usual and the shadows beneath her large, dark brown eyes were certainly more pronounced. But inside, Molly knew she was different. Her self-esteem had as good as packed its bag and left with Colin.

Miserable introspection had been her constant companion these last few weeks and she knew her confidence had vanished. Anger, sadness, resentment all vied for each other as she tried to work out how she had got it so wrong. Each time she thought she had some sort of handle on her emotions, she veered another way until now there was just emptiness.

Taking a deep breath, she whispered her mantra to her reflection; *I'll be fine.*

She wasn't sure what would come next, it was almost impossible to contemplate. Her marriage may be over but so much of her identity was connected to Colin. It was odd to be considering a future without him. Occasional moments of optimism surfaced – hope for what the future might bring – but those moments were eclipsed just as quickly by fear.

At times anxiety and regret threatened to spill over but she forced them back down, determined not to give them a voice in her head. Her life with Colin had been dismantled and now she had to somehow reassemble her life on her own.

The walls had started to close in on her and she knew she had to make a decision. Selling the house was the only option – she certainly couldn't stay here, not now. The house was ready. Colin's penchant for minimalism had ensured Phil Spencer's top tip for selling – depersonalise and declutter – had been easy to achieve. No doubt a few eyebrows would be raised tomorrow when a For Sale sign was hammered into the small patch of clipped grass that constituted their front garden. There had been something liberating about handing over a set of keys to the estate agent's, entrusting them with the viewings. The young estate agent had all but rubbed his hands together when she'd given him the instruction, no doubt anticipating his commission thanks to the recently published league table which had put their house in the catchment area for one of the best performing schools in the country.

Molly checked, perhaps for the fiftieth time that day, her holdall sitting by the front door ready to go tomorrow. Hopefully she'd remembered everything she needed for the next few weeks. Now that her temping job had ended, she was free to embark on her summer escape, as she had taken to calling it.

A whole summer lay ahead of her and apart from selling the house she had made no other decisions. Something about it felt seismic, a sense she was on the cusp of change. This time tomorrow she'd be at West Sands Guest House and she couldn't wait.

# Chapter Two

It may have been June and technically summer but that had never stopped the clouds sweeping in from the Atlantic and unleashing their load onto the west of Scotland and today was no different. Molly hated motorway driving, even more so in wet conditions, and her hands gripped the steering wheel tightly as she concentrated on the road ahead. Huddled in her faithful little red Ford, she stayed in the slow lane, silently cursing every time a lorry thundered by and sent spray lashing onto her window screen.

Earlier that morning she had slipped out of the house, locked the front door and driven out of the quiet cul-de-sac without looking back. In a few hours she'd be at West Sands Guest House in St Andrews and once again, she thanked her lucky stars the way things had worked out.

Molly had resisted running to her parents no matter how effusive she knew their welcome would be – that was assuming they even had room for her in their bijou apartment overlooking Palmira's golf course which was proving to be a very popular destination for friends and family to visit.

Molly's parents had waited for her to finish university before selling the family home in Glasgow where Molly had grown up and retiring to Portugal. Molly had in effect gone from living with her parents to living with Colin. This was her first time flying-solo as it were – albeit not by choice – and she needed to prove to herself as well as to them that she could stand on her own two feet.

She couldn't imagine anything sadder than having your divorced daughter barge in on your well-earned retirement. The thought of facing them, of seeing the disappointment in their faces was something she was quite willing to delay. Her fear was that she would somehow simply crumple and lose herself under their love and attention.

The truth was, Molly felt ashamed. Her happily married and loving parents would somehow reinforce her guilt and shame that she had failed to make her marriage work. She didn't want the fretting and the looks of concern – disrupting their lives would only make her feel worse.

Instead Molly had turned to her brother Stuart. After leaving the family home in Glasgow, he had completed his PhD at Oxford University and had then taken a job lecturing history at Manchester University.

Imparting the news of Colin's affair had produced a few choice expletives from her usually softly spoken brother before he shared his own news which had unexpectedly provided her with a welcome reprieve from agonising about her future – for the next few weeks anyway.

An old friend from his Oxford days had recently started work at St Andrews University, and had contacted Stuart regarding a job lecturing history and he had jumped at the chance. When they were younger, Molly and Stuart had spent a few holidays in St Andrews, mainly to accommodate their parents' love of golf and Molly knew Stuart had always coveted a move to Scotland's oldest university. He and his wife, Anna had decided to up sticks and move their family from Manchester to Scotland. Anna worked as a freelance software developer and after having a difficult year of her own, was happy to start afresh in the small Scottish town.

His friend from Oxford, Ben Matthews, had recently settled in the town himself and as luck would have it, Ben's wife ran a guest house which they could have until they found somewhere of their own to live.

'Come and stay with us,' he said simply.

Memories of those idyllic holidays flickered happily through Molly's mind. Carefree days before grown-up worries of relationships, careers and, in her case, divorces. Frankly, it sounded so perfect she could have wept but she sought reassurance she wouldn't be in the way.

'In the way? Are you kidding? We can always do with an extra pair of hands and the kids would love to see you. There's loads of room and Mum and Dad will be coming for some of the time too.'

Knowing her parents would be there had clinched it for Molly. Stuart and the family would provide a welcome distraction and ensure she wasn't the sole focus of their attention and hopefully by the time she saw them, she'd be feeling stronger.

Molly had hung up, relief filtering through her body. The next few weeks lay ahead enticingly empty, hopefully giving her the time and space she so badly needed to decide what came next. Or perhaps not to think at all. Simply to be herself again and not Colin's wife – she needed to try and remember what that felt like.

Now, as Molly continued to drive eastwards across the country, the rain eventually stopped and the clouds parted to make way for a pale blue sky. A good omen, she thought, feeling her shoulders loosen. She flicked on the radio, humming along to the music, feeling her spirits lift at the thought of the guest house by the sea filled with noise and family.

Soon she was passing through little fishing villages, navigating her way through narrow, windy roads and looking out onto sandy beaches and picturesque harbours. Approaching St Andrews, Molly slowed down, recognising the skyline of the grand, stately university buildings and other familiar landmarks of the town.

Molly had been delighted when Stuart had told her the guest house was at West Sands beach. Slowing down as she drew closer to the house, Molly let out a little gasp. A rather grand-looking Victorian house, it sat opposite a sweep of white sand with the sea stretching into the distance. Dark green ivy tumbled down the soft redbrick walls and the windows glittered in the afternoon sunshine. Terracotta pots brimming with small creamy flowers stood either side of the glossy blue front door.

The wheels crunched on the gravel driveway as Molly brought the car to a halt and she smiled, seeing the small welcoming party that had formed at the door to meet her. She felt her heart squeeze with love for them. Stuart lifted a hand and waved to her, his other arm around his wife's shoulders. Seeing Stuart and Anna standing there reminded Molly of her parents. Like them they looked so happy and made it look easy – they did marriage well in this family, all except her it seemed. If she didn't love them so much it would be easy to feel envious. She was barely out of the car before they swooped down on her with hugs and kisses.

'You're here!'

Wrapped in the warmth of Anna's embrace, Molly's suddenly shaky equilibrium was painfully tested but she swallowed down the tears that threatened, determined not to lose it now. Luckily the moment passed as her brother pulled her in for a gruff-like brotherly hug.

'Good to see you, little sis.' Molly grinned up at him, so happy to see her brother. At thirty-five, he was six years older than Molly. Growing up there had never been any rivalry between the siblings even though Stuart had given Molly enough reason for there to be one, at least academically. Instead she was proud of her brother's straight A record and subsequent offers from the country's top universities.

Tall, dark and totally oblivious to the effect his looks had on women, Molly had assumed the role of protector, vetting who was suitable. Operating on the premise that no one was good enough for her brother, Molly had been prepared not to like Anna, the first girl Stuart had ever brought home. But any fears Molly had were quashed within seconds of meeting her and she had pretty much charmed the whole family.

Not only had she been good for her brother – she had lovingly pulled him back from a life of crumpled corduroy and tweed jackets – she had become a good friend to Molly, too.

Molly turned to her eleven-year-old niece Lily. Wearing jeans and a sparkly T-shirt and sharing her father's reserved nature, she had held back slightly. She gave her aunt a shy look and Molly enveloped her in a hug. Luke, on the other hand, had no such reservations and stood beside Molly grinning up at her.

'Look at you! You've grown!' Molly exclaimed, ruffling his blond hair. Luke held himself tall, beaming a cheeky grin. 'I'm five now,' he announced proudly.

Stuart opened the boot and lifted her bag out. 'Brought your golf clubs, I see?' he chuckled.

'How could I not when I knew I was coming here. Thought I might see if you had time for a game.'

'What and be humiliated? Not likely.'

Molly laughed, shaking her head. 'I'll be totally useless now anyway, I haven't played for so long.'

It had always been a bit of a family joke that Molly was the son their father had always wanted. With his aversion to the great outdoors, Stuart preferred spending his time with his head in a book while Molly would be out tramping the golf course with their father.

Luke suddenly grabbed Molly by the hands, pulling her towards the house excitedly.

'Give Aunt Molly a chance,' Anna chastised him good-naturedly.

And in that moment, as Molly was swept into the house, she couldn't think of a single place she'd rather be.

\*\*\*\*

14

'That was delicious,' Molly said gratefully, feeling nicely full from the paella Anna had made. The crisp Sauvignon Blanc had also gone down a treat. Sitting at the large oak table in the dining room, Molly felt herself start to relax as she caught up with Stuart and Anna.

It had turned into a beautiful evening and the adults smiled, hearing the shrieks of delight floating through the French doors from the garden where Lily and Luke were playing.

'You certainly know the right presents to bring your niece and nephew,' Anna commented sagely.

'Couldn't really go wrong with water guns, could I?' Molly grinned.

Stuart had been bringing Molly up to date about his new job at the university, which to all intents and purposes he'd already started. He and Anna had known for a while now that there was no such thing as long summer holidays for university lecturers and that the academic grindstone never truly stopped.

'I'm working on proposals for a funding initiative and supervising some students completing their final projects. I'm also preparing a workshop on the study of Medieval Scotland,' he explained with his usual enthusiasm as he topped up their glasses.

'Think I get the picture – no rest for the wicked,' Molly teased. 'So you've already met your colleagues?'

'Most of them, they all seem very nice,' he murmured vaguely. Molly smiled to herself. Often suspecting her brother's mind was somewhere in the fifteenth century half the time, she knew that even if his colleagues were awful, he probably wouldn't notice or comment.

With a sigh, Molly sat back in her seat and took a sip of her wine, her eyes sweeping the room. Buttermilk-coloured walls complemented the oak furniture and a large seagrass rug sat on the wooden floor. There was a small side table piled with brochures and local maps for visitors and a small indoor bay tree sat next to a comfy cream wicker armchair. The room oozed comfort and style.

Following her gaze, Anna smiled. 'Isn't this house just perfect?' she said.

Molly had felt it as soon as she stepped into the house earlier: an ambience which seemed to draw you into its warm embrace. And judging by the toy-strewn floor – she'd already had to avoid stepping on Luke's cars – the children had made themselves very much at home.

'So it's Ben's wife Eva that runs the guest house, is that right?' Molly asked.

Anna nodded. 'She used to run this house as a bed and breakfast but she lives next door now with Ben and her son Jamie. Obviously she knew our situation and she explained that as this was her first summer renting out the whole house, a longer let suited her perfectly. So, we've been so lucky to get it for as long as we need.'

'A case of good timing.'

'Definitely. Eva came round and had a coffee and stayed chatting for ages. She's just set up her own interior design business and her son Jamie is a year older than Lily so she'll be going to the same school as him.'

'Ben teaches physics, is that right?'

Stuart nodded. 'He's been showing me around the university and introducing me to a few people which has been really helpful.'

Molly nodded with a smile. 'Well, I'm glad to hear it's all working out so well.'

'And of course, as long as we are here, you can stay. There's no immediate rush for you to go back is there?' Stuart lifted an eyebrow.

Molly took a moment to gather her thoughts.

'Well, I'll have to deal with the house sale at some point but it's only just gone on the market. Then after that, I'll need to find somewhere to live – I was thinking I might rent for a while. And of course, I'll need to find another job.' Damn that little wobble in her voice. She cleared her throat, noticing the small exchange of glances between her brother and Anna.

Molly knew they had been concerned about her and she appreciated being able to speak them but she'd done enough sobbing down the phone. She'd told them she'd love to visit them in St Andrews but on the proviso there was to be no post-mortem of her marriage. She really didn't want to rake over the ashes of her marriage. She'd vowed she wouldn't let her newly divorced status intrude on their family holiday and so she drew in a deep breath, determined not to falter. *I'll be fine.*

'We just wish there was something more we could do.'

'Being here with you now is enough,' Molly said firmly. She gave Stuart a pointed look. 'And you don't need to tiptoe around me. You've never done it before and don't you dare start now,' she told him. Stuart held his hands up in mock surrender, lightening the mood.

'Okay, but remember I am still your big brother despite the fact you've bossed me about your whole life.'

'That's because you needed it for your own good,' Molly countered with a grin.

'Anyway, I'll have Mum for back up when she arrives.'

Molly rolled her eyes. 'You always were her blue-eyed boy,' she said affectionately. 'Do we know exactly when they're arriving?' she asked.

'Dad managed to get them tickets for the last day's play of the tournament at the old course in a couple of weeks.'

Molly took a gulp of wine, her mind calculating how long she had to shore up her defences before facing her mother's barrage of concern.

A sudden high-pitched scream from outside indicated delight had turned to disaster and five seconds later Lily marched in followed by a sheepish looking Luke. They were both drenched.

'Mum, he squirted the water at my face on purpose and hit my eye.' Lily was close to tears, her face puce with indignation. Anna sighed, automatically rising from her seat to mediate.

'Remember I said no faces, Luke? Say sorry to Lily, please.'

'Sorry, Lily,' he parroted. Then with all remorse instantly forgotten he turned to Molly. 'Is Uncle Colin not coming to see us anymore?'

'Shut up, Luke.' Lily scowled.

The simplicity and unexpectedness of the question took Molly by surprise, as did the tears that suddenly welled in her eyes.

'Right you two. Upstairs for showers now!' Stuart interjected. 'Tell you what,' he said, turning to his wife and Molly. 'Why don't you two take a stroll? Go and have a drink somewhere and I'll deal with these two little horrors.'

Molly wasn't sure she was in the mood to go out. All her recent interactions with people had been confined to work colleagues and even having a meal with Stuart and Anna had felt slightly alien. But Anna was clapping her hands together, rushing over to plant a kiss on Stuart's cheek.

'Come on, Molly, let's go before he changes his mind.'

After a quick freshen up – and in Molly's case a few private moments to compose herself – the two women were soon strolling along the cobbled streets, the setting sun casting the last of its golden rays over the town. Most of the shops had closed but there were plenty of people milling around, choosing where to have their evening meal.

Anna turned her head towards Molly. 'Sorry about Luke earlier. We didn't say anything to him but he must have overheard us talking.' She grimaced.

Molly waved her hand indicating it was nothing. 'Don't worry. Besides, he's only five. It's not his fault.'

'I understand you don't want to talk about things, but you are okay? Stuart has been worried about you.'

'I know,' Molly sighed, hating the thought of her family worrying about her.

She frowned, trying to remember the last time Colin had even seen her family, realising he had managed to extricate himself from any recent gatherings. She'd always hoped Colin and Stuart would have bonded but it had never happened.

'Colin and Stuart never did have much in common, did they?' she commented now.

'They were very different people,' Anna said diplomatically. 'As long as you know we're here for you.'

'Thanks. But honestly I'm fine,' Molly replied, forcing a bright smile.

Steering away from the main street and down a little lane, they found a rustic-looking pub and were soon ensconced at a table surrounded by the hum of conversation and the occasional peals of laughter erupting from a group sitting at one of the larger tables.

'Cheers.' They clinked glasses.

'You're going to love it here,' Molly enthused. 'What a great place for the children to grow up.'

Anna made a face, picking up her glass. 'I'm not sure Lily would agree with you, she's very unsure about the whole move.'

Molly had noticed Lily seemed a bit quiet, even for her. 'Is she really worried?'

'She's a bit sensitive just now – I think that's why she over-reacted with Luke earlier. It's fair to say she resents us for dragging her away from all her old friends to a new school. I've tried to tell her everything will be fine but she's so shy and you know how cruel children can be.'

'I don't suppose anyone wants to be the new kid at school, do they?'

Molly's heart went out to her niece. She knew all the reassurances in the world wouldn't stop Lily worrying about her first day at a new school not knowing anyone. 'Hopefully being in a small community will make it easier for her to make new friends.'

Anna agreed. 'That's why I'd like to try and get a new house sorted as soon as possible – I think being settled before the children start school will help. Plus if I stay in the guest house too long I'll feel like I'm on a permanent holiday and that won't do at all.'

Molly looked affectionately at her sister-in-law. Her petite frame, elfin-cut blonde hair and large blue eyes belied the strength of the woman underneath. As well as being one of the smartest people Molly had ever met, she was one of the most driven with a work ethic that put lesser mortals to shame.

Anna had met Stuart when he had moved to work in Manchester. She worked for a high-tech company and did amazing things with computers that Molly didn't understand. After the children were born she set up as a freelance software developer and was so successful that now people came to her. She didn't do rest. For as long as Molly had known her, Anna had always been involved in some job, working long hours. And being your average everyday super woman, she appeared to balance it all.

Except looking at her now, Molly could see tiredness etched on her features, a lack of her customary sparkle. But then it was hardly surprising, she'd had a horrible eighteen months. She had lost both her parents and as an only child she'd taken the full brunt of the dealing with the illnesses that had claimed first her mother and then her father. Molly had met Anna's parents at the odd family occasion. They had been lovely and Molly could only imagine how painful it must be for Anna to lose them both.

'What about you, how have you been?' Molly asked her now.

'Oh, I'm fine,' she replied breezily.

'You don't have a job on at the moment, do you?'

'No, I'm taking a few weeks off for the move.'

'I'm glad to hear it. I know things have been difficult but hopefully this will be a fresh start for all of you,' Molly encouraged.

Anna attempted a smile but didn't quite make it.

Molly looked at her with concern. 'Are you sure you're all right?'

Anna sighed and looked down. 'I know moving here is the right thing. It's just the thought of starting over and meeting new people can seem a bit daunting I suppose. I've always lived in a city with Mum and Dad close by and I suppose I miss them more than I could have thought possible.' She lifted her hands then let them drop in her lap.

Molly reached over and squeezed her arm. 'It's going to take time.'

Anna stared into her glass before taking a deep breath. 'You're right.' She sat up straight, giving herself a shake. 'And as you say, coming here is a new start. Will we have one more before we go? This is your first night here and we better make the most of it. I'll make them large.'

Molly watched Anna make her way to the bar. She knew the alcohol had lowered her defences but it was still odd to see Anna, usually so strong and confident, sounding despondent.

She could only imagine how difficult it must be for Anna and wished she could find words to give her comfort. At least she knew she could be here for her and vowed there and then to do as much as possible to help in any way she could. It also showed her that her decision not to unload any of her own woes had been the right thing to do. Anna and Stuart had quite enough to deal with.

Anna appeared brighter as she brought their drinks over and proposed a toast.

'Here's to summer,' she said lifting her glass. 'I'm so glad you came.'

'As long as I'm not in the way.'

Anna shook her head. 'But I will admit, I do have an ulterior motive. I was hoping you'd help me look for houses – you know what Stuart's like. Ask him anything you want about medieval kings but he's not so hot on the merits of south-facing gardens.'

Molly giggled. 'Of course, I'd love to help you.'

'I've already seen an estate agent and got a viewing lined up.'

'That's exciting.'

'It'll be good to get the furniture out of storage and get settled.' Anna drained her glass, her gaze homing in on a group of men sitting across from them. 'Just think of all the nice men out there you could meet now.'

Molly shook her head. 'Not interested.'

'A few dates wouldn't do any harm though, would it?'

Even hearing the word 'date' made Molly feel slightly hysterical. Was that something she was going to have to do in the future? The idea was quite appalling.

'You need to get back out there,' Anna announced, nodding her head.

Molly wasn't sure about much recently – the foundations of her life had shifted – but one thing she did know unequivocally was that she was not interested in relationships, meeting someone, having a fling or anything else man-related.

She grimaced even thinking about it – she was so not ready at all for that. Far too soon and scary.

Another large glass later and, feeling quite pleased with themselves, Molly and Anna started to walk back to the house. Molly had consumed just the right amount of alcohol to put a positive spin on things. Her marriage wasn't a waste of precious years, she would find love again and somehow a career – or at least a job she loved – would miraculously appear. Yes, her life was looking much brighter through a soft-focus alcohol haze.

Anna hiccupped. 'I'm so happy you came.'

'I think you said that already.'

'Did I? Well, I am.'

'Stuart might not be so happy when he sees the state we're in. He'll think I'm a bad influence.' They giggled, linking arms as they stepped out onto the road.

Molly let out a yelp of surprise as car brakes sounded followed by an angry beep behind them. They jumped back on the pavement, Molly catching the striking blue eyes of the driver as he passed by with a shake of his head.

'Well, that was rude,' she said indignantly, managing to totally ignore the fact they had walked onto the road without looking. And laughing, they headed back to the house.

# Chapter Three

Molly opened one eye and groaned. She lay still while her body processed the miseries of her hangover; nausea, pounding head and a dry mouth. Slowly she opened the other eye to see a room full of unfamiliar shapes and shadows and it took her mind a moment to piece together where she was and the reason for her current fragile state.

She had enjoyed last night and it had been good to relax and chat with Anna but getting drunk on her first night probably hadn't been the best idea. She remained motionless, listening for any sounds but thankfully the house was blissfully quiet. She wasn't sure she could cope with noise right now.

Very slowly she sat up and looked around. Her bedroom was one of five in the house and situated at the back of the guest house. When she'd arrived yesterday, Luke had insisted on giving her a tour of the house. Stuart and Anna's room was at the front of the house, a beautiful coastal themed room with duck-egg-blue walls and views of the sea. Another of the bedrooms was painted in pale green with a tartan armchair and a painting of the Cairngorms hanging over the fireplace.

Molly's room was unashamedly feminine with decorative floral wallpaper and cream embroidered bedding. A ceramic lamp and a pot filled with sprigs of purple heather sat on a traditional wooden dressing table in front of the window.

It certainly had to be the prettiest room to have a hangover in, she thought ruefully. Gently peeling back the covers she swung her legs over the side of the bed, eyeing her bag still full of her clothes sitting in the corner of the room. There hadn't really been time to unpack yesterday so that was a job for later. She narrowed her eyes against the daylight as she drew the curtains open. By the looks of the weather she had been right to treat herself to some new summer clothes.

When Molly had decided to sort through her summer wardrobe a few weeks ago, she had become painfully aware all the clothes had been chosen because she knew they would meet with Colin's approval.

For the last couple of years, Colin had been very specific about the holidays they had taken. He had taken to lording it up in five-star resorts, lounging at the pool all day and dining in the best restaurants. Molly hadn't always enjoyed that type of holiday – there were cities and places she dreamed of exploring – but she respected that Colin worked hard and needed his rest and relaxation. Priding himself on his skin being able to turn a particular shade of brown, the focus of the entire day had been rotating his sunbed to follow the sun and the only thing Colin wanted to explore after a hard day's tanning was the bar's cocktail list. Molly's summer clothes, therefore, were suitable for either lounging at the pool during the day or dining in restaurants where the dress code dictated she squeeze herself into formal evening wear.

Gathering up all those clothes, she had folded them neatly into bags and taken them to the charity shop and then taken herself to the shops.

With only herself to please now, she'd indulged in a spree of floaty, casual and feminine clothes – ditsy skirts and flowery dresses, brightly coloured vest tops and shorts, flat sandals – a world away from the restrictive clothes she had poured herself

25

into. She'd also taken the precaution of packing a few jackets and jumpers; this was Scotland, after all.

Feeling mildly better after a hot shower in the en-suite bathroom, she dressed in skinny jeans, a stripy blue and white T-shirt and her comfortable trainers. As she made her way downstairs, a message pinged on her phone explaining why the house was deserted. Stuart's message said that he and Anna had taken the children off for the day to a nearby country park and that they'd bring home fish and chips for dinner. She baulked at the thought of food right now, but texted him back telling them to have a great day and that she'd see them later.

She wandered through the hall and into the front room. The cream walls were bathed in morning sunlight and two large sofas sat either side of a cast-iron fireplace. In one corner a shelved recess held a selection of board games and paperbacks for guests. Molly ran her finger along some of the titles reflecting on how much she liked being here in the guest house. Not just because it was so comfortable and stylish but because of its neutrality after the suffocating atmosphere she'd left behind in her own home. She liked that there were no reminders of Colin or their marriage. She felt free from the confines of her normal life and routines and that suited her. Spotting the title of a book she'd wanted to read for ages she made a mental note to come back for it later. A mug of tea and an early night suddenly sounded very appealing.

In the kitchen Molly saw the scattered remains of breakfast still in evidence and set about tidying up. She washed down the surfaces, wiping away splodges of jam and puddles of milk and put away a huge box of cereal. Once she had finished tidying, she found a glass and as she filled it with cold water, felt a pang of guilt, hoping Anna wasn't feeling as bad as she did. She drank thirstily, thinking how much energy it took to have children. Not that she would mind of course. She knew there was a flip side to all the worry and hard work. There was the love and laughter, both things she hoped to have one day. She sighed, rinsing her glass, not prepared to let her thinking go down that route.

In the meantime, she had the day to herself. The urge to collapse on that lovely squashy sofa was tempting but outside the sunshine beckoned and Molly reckoned a good dose of sea air was just what she needed.

Within minutes she was walking along the cobbled streets, mingling with families and tourists and enjoying the warmth of the sun on her skin. The last time she'd been here was as a girl with her parents and now she absorbed her surroundings with new eyes. The quaint, charming town with its eclectic mix of shops and cafés made the city feel a million miles away.

Out of nowhere Colin zipped into her mind and she wondered what he was doing, if he was happy with his new life. The only communication between them had been the odd email about the divorce proceedings. How formal and final it all sounded.

She took a deep breath of fresh air, determined not to let thoughts of her ex-husband infiltrate her mind. Instead, she tried to allow a sense of tranquillity wash over her. She was here to think about the future, not the past. For today though, she simply wanted to explore and get a sense of her surroundings.

Heading towards the water she took a few moments to admire the fine grandeur of the Royal and Ancient Golf Club before continuing through the leafy medieval streets where many of the university buildings were housed. She walked through St Mary's quadrangle, stopping to read the plaque by the decayed stump of a hawthorn tree which, according to legend, Mary Queen of Scots had planted on one of her many visits to the town. Molly smiled, knowing how much her brother was going to love this. The historical setting would be a dream for him.

She kept walking, following a path between the golf course and the beach which snaked along the coastline until it eventually started to turn inland. She crossed over a footbridge and then upwards through a wooded glen, pausing at a little burn trickling down the hill.

Molly enjoyed the peace and let her thoughts wander until she had to stop to catch her breath. Standing with her hands on her hips, she looked back the way she had come and although it afforded her a lovely view of the town, she realised she had walked much further than she had intended. She didn't suppose the hangover was helping but she couldn't blame that entirely for her current state which was now decidedly weak and wobbly. There was nothing like a good hike to show how unfit you were, she thought wryly, feeling the full impact of her recent car-reliant existence. With her slightly alarming heart rate and jelly legs, she promised herself there and then to try and improve her fitness.

Still, the pain was worth it because now she was surrounded by trees and lush greenery. It was so tranquil, almost like being in the middle of an enchanted forest. She was glad of the shade provided by the trees and wished she'd had the sense to bring water with her.

She noticed a path and, walking towards it, spotted a carved wooden sign announcing The Drumloch Inn lay ahead. Very fortuitously, the sign also indicated food and beverages being served all day. Molly, quite weak with fatigue and dehydration by now, felt herself sag with relief. The thought of a seat and drink sounded heavenly.

The inn, almost hidden by shrubs and trees, was a charmingly pretty two-storey stone building with wisteria growing up the walls. Baskets spilling over with purple fuchsias graced both sides of the double front door and, as she walked through them, Molly had the sense of being in a rather grand country house.

Inside, the floor was carpeted in tweed and the walls panelled in dark wood. A large vase of lilies sat on a mantelpiece above an open fireplace and a beautifully ornate chandelier hung from the ceiling.

Molly approached the small reception desk where a lady sat.

Molly placed her to be in her sixties although her stylish bob and immaculate make-up gave her an ageless glamour.

'Good morning, can I help you?' the lady asked. Her glasses were perched on top of her head, reminding Molly of her own mother and her smile was so warm and genuine Molly immediately felt at ease.

'Hello. I'm not a guest here but is it all right if I sit and have a drink. I saw the sign—'

'Of course!' the lady gushed. She stood up, knocking a sheaf of papers to the floor.

'Sorry, I'm all fingers and thumbs today. We've got a new computer system installed and I'm still working my way through this manual…' She gestured to the offending documents which she had now retrieved from the floor. Straightening up and looking slightly flustered, she smiled again. 'Now, where were we? Come with me and I'll show you where you can have a seat.'

Molly followed her through to a lounge area of seating in front of arched windows which looked out onto an expanse of rolling greenery. Molly took a seat on one of the sofas, grateful to be off her aching feet and was soon perusing the drinks menu that the lady had given her.

Molly ran her eye down the selection of drinks on offer, surprised and delighted by the choice; hand-pressed apple juice, traditional ginger beer, elderflower and cucumber or berry and mint refreshers. She eventually decided on a sparkling rhubarb and after a few minutes the lady returned with the drink in a tall glass, served on a little coaster with a serviette.

Molly took a drink and sat back with a sigh of appreciation. Feeling slightly conspicuous as the solitary customer, she glanced around. Tartan and gingham sofas, comfy chairs and dark wooden tables adorned with small vases of flowers created a relaxed, cosy ambience. There was another fireplace and a small brass-topped bar tucked discreetly in the corner.

After a while the lady came over to check if Molly needed anything else.

'I'm Judy, the owner here. Do you mind if I join you for a little while?'

'Not at all.' Molly smiled, indicating the seat beside her. 'I'm Molly Adams, it's nice to meet you.'

The lady eased herself down gracefully onto the seat and Molly instantly sat up straighter.

'How was your drink?' she asked.

'I really enjoyed it,' Molly answered truthfully. 'It was delicious and very refreshing.'

The lady tilted her head, looking pleased. 'Thank you. It was one of my creations.'

'You make the drinks yourself?'

'I do. I source all the ingredients locally and then I have great fun concocting all the different flavours up.'

Molly was impressed.

'I have an excellent local cook who comes in to do the evening meals and breakfast but drinks are my speciality,' Judy explained. 'I was a flight attendant and I think all those years serving up drinks to passengers must have rubbed off on me.'

'Well, it was delicious,' Molly reiterated.

'Are you here on holiday?'

Molly explained about her brother coming to live in St Andrews with his family.

'I'm sure they'll be very happy here.'

Molly nodded in agreement and then admitted how she had stumbled on the inn by accident. 'It's such a lovely location here although I hadn't realised I had walked so far.'

Judy pursed her lips. 'We are a bit off the beaten track here. Which can be a good and bad thing. Once people find us, they love it and we have a lot of repeat business. Other times, being so far from the town can put people off.'

'It's a very romantic setting.'

'It is, isn't it? We only have six rooms – four doubles, one single and one family room so it's mostly couples who book.'

'How long have you owned it for?'

'My husband and I bought this place six years ago. I was a flight attendant and he was a pilot and we fell very much in love and it was always our dream to own a place like this. We had ten very happy years together but unfortunately he passed away four years ago.'

'I'm so sorry. That must be difficult for you.'

'It can be.' She gave a small smile. 'But the business keeps me busy which is good. Especially now the golf school is open again.' She nodded her towards the window.

Molly gazed out of the window and only now did it dawn on her she had in fact been looking out at a golf course. In the far distance Molly could make out a flag marking one of the course's holes.

'That's a golf course over there?'

'Yes, that's Drumloch golf course and though you can't see through the trees, there's a golf school and range as well.'

Molly perked up with interest.

'It was run down for a while,' Judy continued. 'But it's recently been bought over by two golf professionals and I know they've got plans for the place.'

'I might take a walk over and have a look.'

'Do you play golf?' Judy asked.

'I used to play a bit with my father,' she replied. 'What about you, do you play?'

'Me? Goodness, no. Never understood the mystery of chasing a white ball about,' she laughed. 'Although George played and always wanted me to learn so we could play together.'

'Well, I should probably get going,' Molly said, conscious she had the return walk to undertake.

'Why don't you go and have a look at the golf course now?' Judy suggested.

31

Molly hesitated.

'It really is only a few minutes' walk. When you leave here, turn right and you'll see a tree-lined path. Just follow it and when you come to a little picnic area with a couple of wooden tables, you're practically there.'

'How much do I owe you?' Molly asked, getting to her feet.

'On the house,' Judy insisted. 'I've enjoyed meeting you and it's been lovely to have a little chat.'

'Thank you, I've enjoyed it too,' Molly replied, surprised by how easy she had found talking to the older lady. Outside in the sunshine again and feeling rejuvenated, Molly debated with herself whether to go and check out the golf school now or come back another day.

When she had known she was coming to St Andrews Molly had dug out her set of clubs languishing in the attic collecting dust. Now she hoped to have some practice at one of the ranges and maybe persuade her brother to have a game.

Both her parents had played but it had been her father in particular who had passed on his love of the game to Molly. When she'd been a little girl, Molly hadn't been interested in dance classes, swimming or any of the other activities on offer but had taken to hitting the ball. One day her dad had taken her to a range and she could still recall the look of surprise on his face when, with apparent ease, she smacked a ball a hundred yards down the middle of the fairway. After that, she was his caddy whenever possible and when she was older she played with him at their local club.

Her father was a quiet, thoughtful man and not one to talk much but it became their thing to do together and some of her happiest memories were of the two of them on the course together. She sighed thinking of those times. Sometimes the simplest things really were the best.

At this time of year Molly knew all the golf facilities in town would be busy which was why this location was so appealing. She could see the little path now. Overhung with trees and surrounded by wildflowers, it almost seemed to beckon her. Molly made an instant decision – she was this close, she may as well check it out.

After a few minutes she passed the picnic area that Judy had mentioned and then the golf school came into view – a modern, timber frame building with dark wood cladding.

To one side Molly could see the practice range which consisted of a row of covered bays and to the other side was a small putting green. Further away and set amidst the rolling hills, she could see the golf course perched on the rocky shores of the bay with the North Sea as its backdrop. The sun beamed down and sparkled on the water below and Molly took a moment to appreciate the rugged beauty of her surroundings.

She pushed the door open into a reception area which was basically a large room with a few doors leading off it. There was a small counter and a couple of chairs beside a table with a few golf magazines scattered on top.

A tall, gangly boy aged about twenty wearing a tracksuit came bounding over, introduced himself as Kenny and asked how he could help.

'I'd like to come the range one day,' Molly told him. 'Do I need to book in advance?'

The boy shook his head. 'You can turn up any time – but it's empty right now if you'd like to play, I can get you set up?

Molly hesitated for a heartbeat and then decided why not? A little surge of excitement shot through her, it had been so long since she'd played or practised.

The boy helped to get the bucket full of golf balls and, as she didn't have her own clubs with her, gave her a selection of practice clubs to choose from. After thanking him, Molly made her way to the furthest away bay.

It felt odd to be holding a golf club again. She rolled her neck and loosened her shoulders before she started, her father's voice in her head. *Straight back, knees flexed and head steady.*

She took a few tentative shots to warm up, some more successful than others. Molly knew that playing golf wasn't like riding a bike. If you didn't practice, you lost the feel for it. And that was why she wanted to try and use this time because she knew she could be a fairly decent player and with that came confidence – something she was sorely lacking at the moment.

It all came back to her why she loved it so much. The focus it required, the satisfaction of striking the ball. Soon she was enjoying herself, getting into her stride and finding that hitting the ball was quite therapeutic. Considering she had a hangover and it was a few years since she'd hit a ball, she was feeling quite pleased with herself.

After several minutes of hitting the ball Molly heard a door opening and glanced up to see a man coming through one of the doors. Disappointed her solitude had been broken and not relishing the prospect of an audience, she kept her head down hoping he would go away. She lined up her next ball and for some unfathomable reason gave her hips a little wiggle in an attempt to look casual.

Swinging the club perhaps a little too enthusiastically, she caught the edge of the ball with an almighty thwack and watched helplessly as it ricocheted off the roof and rebounded hitting her on the head.

'Ouch!'

Molly stood stunned for a moment, hoping it had sounded worse than it was. She brought her fingers to her head but apart from a small lump forming there didn't seem to be any other damage.

Out the corner of her eye, Molly could see her little commotion had caused the man to look up. Silently willing for him not to come over she kept her head down, but it was too late – he was already making his way towards her.

'Are you all right?'

Molly looked up upon hearing the deep voice.

'Mmm? Oh, yes I'm fine.' She managed a little laugh but couldn't stop a furious blush flooding her cheeks. They regarded one another for a moment and Molly's heart dipped as she recognised the driver who'd made the emergency stop for her and Anna last night. She cringed inwardly, dropping her gaze. She decided ignorance was the best plan and just hoped he wouldn't recognise her.

'Are you sure you're okay? Do you need someone to look at your head?' he asked looking at her with concern.

'No, honestly. I didn't feel a thing,' she lied, beginning to feel uncomfortable under his scrutiny.

'Have you been to a golf range before?'

Molly frowned. 'Lots of times actually,' she replied defensively, not liking the feeling he was assessing her in some way.

'Try to take care then, we don't want anyone hurting themselves.'

Molly bristled that his concern was now bordering on admonishment and wished he'd just go away. Perhaps sensing her irritation, he managed to impart a perfunctory smile. Something about his manner was distinctly reserved, almost as if he wasn't sure he wanted to be there. Or worse, didn't want her to be there. She hoped he wasn't one of the sexist ignoramuses who thought women shouldn't play golf because if he was she might just swing the club in his direction. Molly was just wondering exactly who he was when he introduced himself.

'I'm Tom Kennedy, one of the golf professionals here.'

So that explained his concern. He was probably making sure she wasn't going to make some sort of injury claim. And knowing he was a professional sportsman certainly explained his physique and healthy, outdoorsy look. He held out a hand for her to shake, her hand feeling tiny in his large, firm grip.

'I'm Molly Adams.'

'As long as you're all right, then,' he said gruffly.

Even in her slightly inebriated state last night, some part of

35

Molly's brain had registered the handsome driver as he passed. Sober and up close her assessment was the same. In fact, he was very handsome, she observed now, her eyes taking in his piercing blue eyes, short dark hair and square jaw. He was tall with powerful-looking shoulders and Molly felt a ripple of attraction run through her. Clearly the alcohol was still fizzing its way through her system.

Seemingly reassured she wasn't about to pass out he took a step back and leaned against the partition board, his large frame filling the small space. Molly's eyes drifted to his tanned forearms and swallowed hard.

'Are you here on holiday in St Andrews?'

She nodded. 'My brother and his family have taken a guest house for the summer so I'm staying with them for a few weeks.'

'Do you play much golf?' he asked.

Molly got the sense he was trying to appear friendly but it wasn't coming easily to him. If he was one of the new owners he might want to brush up on his people skills.

'I was captain for my local club's girls' team and I've played some great courses actually.'

She saw his eyebrow arch in surprise. Great, next she'd be saying she was best friends with Tiger Woods. 'I mean I've never played seriously or anything and I haven't played for ages so obviously I'm out of practice,' she back-tracked desperately, suddenly finding her feet fascinating to look at. Reluctantly she dragged her gaze up, detecting the tiniest flicker of amusement in his eyes.

'Are you planning on any more golf while you're here?'

'Hopefully. Just some practice at the range. See if I can drag my brother out for a game.' Molly wondered if he was really interested or just going through the motions.

'It's a good course here at Drumloch and it's only nine holes which is ideal if you haven't played for a while.'

'Um, sure, thanks. That's good to know.'

He shifted his weight from one leg to another and Molly detected an almost indiscernible discomfort as he did so. She sensed a suppressed energy from him, something she couldn't put her finger on and despite herself she felt her curiosity piqued by the man with the intense eyes standing in front of her. She gave herself a shake, deciding it was definitely time for her to go.

'I should be leaving,' she said, beginning to gather her things.

'You really are okay? You're not hurt?' he checked again.

'Definitely not hurt, thanks.'

He looked at her while running a hand across the back of his neck, appearing slightly awkward. 'Hope to see you again then.'

Molly smiled though doubted he meant that. She turned and walked away, noticing her hangover had totally disappeared.

# Chapter Four

A few days later Molly and Anna were on their way to a house viewing but got distracted passing a pretty café called The Coffee Hut, with blue and white striped awnings hanging over the window.

'We've got time, haven't we?' Molly looked at Anna, her stomach already rumbling in anticipation. After a quick glance at her watch, Anna agreed it was a splendid idea. Inside was warm and cosy, scents of coffee and baking mingling in the air and they stood at the counter for a few minutes trying to choose from all the delicious baking on display. Anna finally settled on a home-made scone with raspberry jam while Molly opted for the lemon shortbread.

They settled at one of the tables by the window, taking in their surroundings. The café was busy with customers, some chatting and some hunched over laptops. Apart from one exposed brick wall the others were painted different colours and covered in artwork.

The past couple of days had slipped by pleasantly. It was only after a few restorative nights' sleep at the guest house that Molly appreciated just how badly she'd been sleeping at home. After Colin left she had considered sleeping in the spare room but had obstinately remained in the marital king-size bed. She had piled pillows where her husband used to lie and on nights when sleep wouldn't come they proved to be very useful for pummelling.

Luke and Lily were looking rosy-cheeked and healthy. They had been swimming and had enjoyed a day at the aquarium. The spiders, seals and meerkats had gone down very well, especially with Luke. Molly knew what an important time it was for Stuart, Anna and the children; there was a lot for them all to adjust to and so she'd tried to help out as much as possible. She had also wanted to give them time as a family and so had taken herself off now and again. In theory she was supposed to be addressing her thoughts to the future but her thinking only got so far before she became overwhelmed and apart from a few tentative job searches she had to admit she hadn't done much.

A waitress set down their order, which looked delicious, and Molly took a bite of the moist, crumbly shortbread, rolling her eyes in appreciation while Anna poured tea from a white ceramic teapot into pretty matching cups.

'So tell me about this house we're going to see,' she asked Anna. The agreed plan was for Anna and Molly to do the initial viewings and if Anna liked any, then Stuart and the children would come for the second viewings.

'Hold on, I'll tell you,' Anna replied, wiping her hands on a cream napkin and reaching for her phone.

'Willow Cottage. A traditional stone built detached villa situated in a leafy street…needs some modernisation…' She scrolled down her phone. 'Oh, it's actually further away than I thought. We might have a bit of a walk.'

Molly nodded, finishing her biscuit. 'Sounds interesting.'

'Maybe – not sure about the modernisation though, that could mean it's basically falling down.'

As they continued to scrutinise the house details, a woman who Molly had seen earlier behind the counter appeared at their table. Her mass of red curls and the smock dress she wore with

39

chunky silver jewellery gave her a bohemian air and Molly was struck by how relaxed and comfortable she appeared.

'Morning, ladies.' She smiled. 'I just wanted to check everything is okay for you?'

'Everything's great, thanks,' Anna replied.

'I'm Freya, the owner here and that's my husband Jack.' She waved her hand in the direction of the man behind the counter whose return wave suggested he was used to this little scenario. Anna explained about moving to the town and staying at West Sands Guest House.

'Oh, Eva is a good friend of mine. She and Ben are such a lovely couple. We started our businesses around the same time.'

'How long ago was that?'

Freya narrowed her eyes thinking. 'Let's see, that must be about nine years now.'

Molly's eye had been caught by all the lovely artwork – mostly seascapes – covering the walls of the café.

'Who does all the paintings?'

'I do,' Freya replied.

'Gosh, you find time to do all the paintings as well as run the café?' Anna asked in awe.

'To be fair, it's Jack who runs the café mostly so that I have time to do my painting. But it wasn't always like that. We were both working in Edinburgh, not seeing much of each other and not really happy. My dream was always to be able to paint but of course it's not easy to make a living from it. So we took a gamble and bought this place. We're never going to be million-aires, but in terms of happiness and seeing each other there's no comparison.'

Molly listened, wondering what it would be like to work beside your husband. Freya and Jack certainly looked happy, she thought, like a proper team working together.

'So no regrets leaving the city?' Anna asked with interest.

'None at all. It's a lovely place to live. The university and the

40

golf are obviously the main attractions, although it's quieter in winter – and much colder. And if I want a city fix I can go to Dundee or Edinburgh easily.'

Freya swung her head round at the sound of the little bell above door announcing the arrival of more customers.

'I'd better get back to work before Jack starts giving me the evil eye. I have an exhibition for my paintings and the opening reception is on Sunday afternoon at the Red Easel Gallery in the main street. You and your family are very welcome. It's very relaxed and I'd love to see you there.'

After saying goodbyes and heading back outside, Anna glanced at her watch. 'We'd better get a move on or we're going to be late,' she said, marching ahead.

They were both slightly red-faced and out of breath when they finally arrived, their unscheduled tea break making them slightly late.

'This looks lovely,' Molly remarked as they rounded the corner into a lane where there was a row of pretty cottages nestled amongst the trees with open fields stretching behind.

'Which one is it?'

'Probably that one with the woman waiting outside.'

The woman – whose shiny, blonde hair and flawless make-up made Molly feel a bit crumpled – was indeed the estate agent waiting for them.

'Good afternoon, I'm Lisa Hamilton.'

'I'm so sorry we're late, we lost track of time,' Anna offered apologetically.

'We do have another viewing booked for immediately after you but hopefully that shouldn't be a problem.' Molly thought she might have seen a tiny flicker of irritation cross the woman's face before she returned to her professional smile.

Anna and Molly followed her through the front door and, despite the warmth of the day, the house immediately felt damp and unforgiving.

'As you'll see, the property does require a fair amount of work. It's been empty for several months due to legal reasons. The owner passed away some time ago in hospital and the only family live in Australia which has slowed things down as the solicitor is handling the sale. I'll be honest, the work has put people off.'

Molly couldn't gauge Anna's reaction but knew this was exactly the type of house she would like for herself one day.

A small entrance vestibule led into the hallway where Molly could see original parquet flooring hidden under several layers of grime. The living room was light and spacious or at least Molly knew it could be – you just had to see past the peeling wallpaper and patches of damp. All the original features were there, just waiting for someone's love and patience to restore them to their former glory. Even though it was a good size, there was a lovely cottagey feel to it. It needed masses of work but Molly could see the potential right away.

Once they had been shown all the rooms, the estate agent left them to have a look around by themselves. Unable to help herself, Molly succumbed to a little daydreaming, allowing herself to imagine all the things she would do.

Anna it seemed, didn't share her vision and Molly saw her worry at her lip, looking disappointed. 'It was unlikely you'd find something straight away,' Molly reasoned, trying to cheer her up.

'I know, I'm being totally unrealistic,' she sighed.

The estate agent, who had been hovering discreetly, now came and asked what they thought of it.

'Mmm, not sure it's right for us to be honest. There's just too much work and I hadn't realised how far from town it is. I don't suppose you have anything else?'

'We were actually given a new instruction yesterday for a property. From what I remember it's in town.'

Anna perked up. 'Do you have the details?'

'If you can wait a moment, I'll have a look,' she replied, starting to scroll through her iPad.

'I'll wait outside,' Molly mouthed to Anna, leaving her to it as she slipped back outside. The small front garden was overgrown and neglected, but in her mind Molly pictured flower-filled borders and little shrubs. She didn't have much clue about gardening but would love to learn one day. A small stepping-stone path led round to the side of the house to a little shed. She imagined pottering about in there on a summer's day while children played. Maybe she could even have a birdbath or a water feature. And maybe she was getting carried away, she realised with a sigh before giving herself a reality check.

She turned at the sound of a car pulling up by the pavement opposite the house and felt her stomach flip as she saw Tom Kennedy unfurling himself out of a car. Again she noticed a slight awkwardness to his movement and assumed he must have an old injury which she guessed was hardly surprising for a professional sportsman. Today his jaw was shadowed by stubble and he was casually dressed in jeans and a blue shirt, the sleeves rolled up enough to show a hint of his forearms. That was strange, he was coming over to the house – his eyes on Molly as he did so.

'Hello.' He sounded mildly surprised.

'Hi.'

They stared at one another for a brief moment, each trying to work out what the other was doing here. He spoke first, a small frown on his forehead.

'Are you here to view the house?'

'Yes. No. I mean, I'm here with my sister-in-law. She and my brother are actually moving to St Andrews and looking for some-where to live so I'm keeping her company. She's just finishing with the estate agent.' She waved her hand towards the house before turning to face him.

'And you – are you viewing it too?' she asked.

He nodded his head in confirmation. 'I've only recently moved to St Andrews myself. I'm living in a hotel temporarily until I find somewhere.'

His tone wasn't exactly conversational and like the first time she had met him, Molly sensed something reserved from him, almost as if he was holding himself back in some way. And like the first time she also felt that same pull of attraction towards him. Perhaps it was some sort of rebound reaction after Colin, she pondered. While on one level she supposed it was good to know her body was functioning normally, it wasn't particularly helpful at this particular moment.

A silence ensued that for some reason Molly felt the need to fill. 'Did you know it takes eight seconds to decide if you're going to buy a house or not?'

He looked at her and quirked an eyebrow. 'I didn't know that.'

'Apparently so.'

He cast his eyes towards the house. 'Looks like there's a lot of work to do.'

'There is but it could be amazing,' Molly enthused unable to help herself. 'If it was me I would totally gut it and start afresh – you know, stamp my own mark on it. It's got so many original features and wait until you see upstairs, where there's two adorable attic bedrooms. I'd probably start with knocking the kitchen and dining room into one big space and then the sash windows could be repaired—' She stopped abruptly, not sure what had possessed her to ramble on like that.

She cleared her throat. 'Anyway, you'll see for yourself soon enough. And between you and me it's not quite what my sister-in-law is looking for so she wouldn't be competition. You know, just in case you do decide to make an offer.'

The smallest of smiles flickered over his lips. 'That's good to know, thanks.'

'No problem,' she replied in a small voice, wondering what on earth was taking Anna so long.

'So um, is your head all right?' she heard him ask.

'Sorry?'

'The ball?' He pointed to her head.

'Oh! Fine, no lasting damage – I think.' She laughed, a tad hysterically. She was beginning to think she might actually have delayed concussion. The way he was looking at her now was making her feel most peculiar.

Just then, Anna came bustling out and made a beeline for them. Molly glanced at her and then at Tom.

'This is Tom Kennedy. He runs the golf school that I've been going to. This is my sister-in-law, Anna.'

Anna's eyes sparkled with interest as she brazenly looked him up and down and Molly had to admit, Tom Kennedy didn't disappoint if you were looking for tall, hunky and handsome. Which she wasn't.

'Nice to meet you,' he said.

'Tom's here to view the house, so we should really get going.' Molly started to move but Anna wasn't going anywhere.

'Really? I don't think it's right for us, but it would make a great family home. Do you have a family Tom? A partner or wife with you…' she asked pleasantly, peering over his shoulder. Molly rolled her eyes wondering if Anna could be any less subtle.

'Tom! Hi, so lovely to see you again.' They all turned at the sound of the estate agent's voice who was coming down the path towards them in what Molly noticed for the first time was a pair of slinky high heels. Now all smiles, she flicked her hair over her shoulder and Molly's mouth fell open slightly at the sudden change in her demeanour. And she was pretty sure who the intended beneficiary of this little display was. Her eyes darted over to Tom to see if it was having an effect – not that it mattered to her – but his expression remained inscrutable. He looked briefly at Molly and nodded, holding her gaze just long enough to send butterflies racing to her stomach before turning to follow the teetering footsteps of Lisa Hamilton.

Well and truly ruffled, Molly took a few hurried paces to catch up with Anna, and after a few calming breaths, turned to her.

'So, what did you think then?'

'I think he's gorgeous.'

'Not him.' Molly let out a puff of air. 'I meant the house.'

'Never mind the house, I might be taking up golf if that's what the instructors look like,' she teased. 'Definitely a bit of the strong silent type thing going on though, I reckon.'

Or the arrogant type, Molly thought to herself as Anna shot her a questioning look.

'Fine, he's very handsome,' she conceded with a shrug. 'But so what? I'm newly divorced unless you forgot and not inclined to think too highly of the male species right now.'

'Exactly. You need to get back out there, have a bit of fun.'

Molly shook her head. 'Not interested.'

'Sometimes these things can just happen though, can't they?' Anna said with a sigh. 'And I thought I detected a little frisson between you.'

'Frisson?' Molly retorted.

'You know, a spark. The way he looked at you.'

Maybe – just maybe – she had felt a little 'frisson' between them too, but Molly wasn't about to admit that to Anna. She had her future to think about and while being alone wasn't appealing, she certainly wasn't about to go jumping into anything quickly, including handsome golfers.

'So, the house? What did you think?' she repeated, steering the conversation onto a safer topic.

'Oh, the house.' Anna tilted her head, thinking. 'Mmm, not quite right. I could see how lovely it could be but I was imagining something bigger with less work to do. The estate agent managed to fix up a viewing for this other house now and has told them we're on our way, is that all right?'

'We'd better get going then,' Molly replied, quickening her pace.

# Chapter Five

Molly frowned at her reflection in the full-length mirror, not sure the running shorts were doing her any favours. Bought months ago with the intention of starting regular exercise that never quite materialised, today she was giving them their first outing on West Sands beach in a bid to improve her fitness levels. She briefly considered changing into something else then shrugged and turned from the mirror. It was insanely early so no one would see her anyway.

She slipped out of the house quietly and headed across to the beach, walking down to the water's edge where the sand was more level. She took a few deep breaths and after some stretches, slowly and tentatively began to jog. The air was crystal clear and the sun had just risen in a sky streaked with a pinkish glow. It was incredibly beautiful and wonderfully peaceful.

Molly was used to having the sights and sounds of the city as a backdrop – cars and buses trundling by, pavements packed with people talking into their phones as they passed. Now she relished the feeling of space and freedom of the deserted beach. It felt almost magical to have it to herself.

She could hardly believe only this time last week she was making the fifty-minute drive across Glasgow to the offices of

Spark Events in the West End. She'd been disappointed when the job had come to an end – not only had she enjoyed the work, it had made her realise how terrible her previous job had been.

After graduating she had worked in the marketing department of a large national insurance company, lured by the job description that promised she'd be involved in creative marketing strategy and customer engagement but the reality had been somewhat different – sitting in a small windowless office amidst a sea of grey filing cabinets, making cups of coffee for a lascivious boss who made her flesh crawl with his endless innuendos and spending hours on the phone asking people how much they spent on life insurance and if they were likely to change it any time soon.

It was a mixed blessing when after five years, she'd been made redundant. Within a week she'd started a year-long temporary position to cover maternity leave at an events company. Molly had taken to it immediately. Whether it was organising a murder mystery weekend for team building, arranging a whisky tasting for a Scottish experience or transferring delegates from their hotel to a conference, she had found something innately satisfying about seeing an event through from the first registration to the last participant leaving. Now she had some experience she was hoping to build on it and find more event work.

After an alarmingly short time Molly became aware her calf muscles were aching and her heart was beating wildly. Identifying a ridge of dunes up ahead, she was determined to reach them without stopping. She upped her speed, pushing herself harder for the final few steps before slowing down and stopping. Breathing heavily, she bent forward, pressing her hand into her side where a painful stitch had taken hold.

'Good morning.'

She raised her eyes to find Tom Kennedy regarding her. Where on earth had he sprung from? She could have sworn the beach had been empty. 'Morning,' she gasped, straightening up.

His jaw was dark with stubble, his hair slightly ruffled and she could see the rise and fall of his broad chest, his T-shirt clinging to the muscles of his shoulders. She couldn't stop her eyes feasting on him, her reaction catching her totally unawares. Now her heart was beating wildly for quite a different reason.

In turn, she felt his eyes skimming over her and she ran a hand over her damp forehead self-consciously, dreading to think what she must look like.

'Don't let me stop you, if you want to keep running,' she said, desperately trying to catch her breath.

He looked down at the strap on his wrist, pressing a button, and Molly wondered how far he'd run. He looked like he could run a marathon without breaking sweat.

'I was almost done anyway.' He surprised her, falling into step beside her as they started to make their way back along the beach. 'I usually have the beach to myself at this time,' he commented.

Molly's head turned sharply at his dry tone. He held her eye for a moment before his face broke into a smile. It was the first genuine smile she'd seen from him and she had to admit it was worth the wait. She smiled back.

'Do you always come running this early?'

His eyes scanned the distance and he nodded. 'This is the best time, I like to come while it's still peaceful.' For some reason that didn't surprise Molly; solitary running on the beach seem to suit him. She followed his gaze.

'Must be lovely to have this on your doorstep,' she agreed before recalling him telling her he'd only recently moved to St Andrews.

'How is your house hunting going?' she asked.

'Slowly,' he admitted ruefully.

'What did you think of Willow Cottage? Did you like it?'

'I did. It needs a lot of work though, as you know.'

'It wasn't right for my sister-in-law, Anna. Too much work for them. Would you be interested in a big project like that?'

'Perhaps.' He shrugged. 'But I'm not sure I'd have the time I'd need to devote to it.'

'The golf school must keep you busy?'

He nodded in confirmation and glanced over at her. 'I've seen you at the range a few times,' he commented.

Molly had looked at some of the other facilities but had been drawn back to Drumloch golf school. She liked that it was away from the hub of the town and was hoping all the walking was doing her city-legs some good. She had seen Tom but had gone out of her way to avoid him. She felt feeble for doing so but their first encounters had left her rattled for some reason. Now she hoped her avoidance tactics hadn't been too obvious.

'I'm not sure I'm improving though,' she admitted.

'You could always have a few lessons?' he suggested lightly.

Molly blinked, trying to imagine a lesson with Tom Kennedy. She doubted she'd be able to concentrate much if the effect his proximity was having on her now was anything to go by.

'Um, maybe,' she replied lightly.

As they continued to walk Molly listened as Tom explained some of the plans he and his business partner Joe had for the school and she was particularly interested in their ideas to encourage women and children. They were thinking up initiatives to move away from the stereotypical old boys' club image of golf.

Molly's curiosity got the better of her. 'Where did you live before here?'

He paused, taking a moment before answering. 'I was playing on the European golf tour for several years so I haven't been settled anywhere.'

Wow. Molly was seriously impressed, she hadn't realised he played golf at that level. She knew enough about golf to know it was only the very best golfers who played on the European tour. She also knew the days of pot-bellied players were long gone and elite players were now mostly muscular, chiselled athletes. And Tom Kennedy certainly fitted into that category.

'The golf school is going to be quite a change then.'

He looked down at the sand, nodding vaguely before seeming keen to change the subject. 'Why is your brother's family moving to St Andrews?'

'He's teaching history at the university. My nephew is five and just starting school and my niece will be starting high school so it's quite a big change for the family.'

He glanced sideways at her. 'We're actually running a junior tournament at Drumloch. We don't want to run before we can walk so it's small scale and strictly for fun.'

'That's a great idea.'

'Your nephew might be a bit young but your niece could certainly enter if she wanted. There's a list in reception at the school if you think she'd be interested.'

Molly nodded thoughtfully. 'I think she would be. She can be a bit shy but I'll certainly put her name down anyway, if that's okay?'

'Of course.'

They had almost reached the end of the beach and the sun had risen fully now. In the near distance a lone dog walker waved over to them and Molly watched as the golden Labrador pulled a stick from the water. West Sands Guest House came into view, looking resplendent in the morning sunshine. Molly pointed it out to Tom and he managed to surprise her again by walking her to the door before saying goodbye.

Molly let herself into the house reflecting how her solo run hadn't gone quite to plan. She hadn't expected to meet anyone, least of all Tom Kennedy. And although she still detected an aloofness from him, he hadn't been entirely unpleasant to speak to. Perhaps she had seen a different side to him. Closing the front door, she wondered if anyone would be awake yet. She thought she should probably have a healthy smoothie but was pretty sure she'd end with coffee.

****

51

Molly smiled as she watched Luke zigzag his way through the university's cloisters, marvelling at his energy. It was a perfect summer's afternoon, a few wispy clouds scudding across the blue sky and the sound of birdsong merging with the lazy buzz of bees hovering around the scented blooms.

Standing on the immaculate lawn in the quadrangle and surrounded by ancient buildings, Molly lifted her eyes to the chapel to admire the blue, green and purple panels of the stain-glass windows sparkling in the sunlight.

The university was holding a garden party for staff, friends and families to mark the end of the graduations and also to thank everyone who had contributed to the recent extension of the university's museum.

Molly sipped her drink soaking up the atmosphere and thinking how relaxed and civilised it all was. People mingling and chatting in small groups while children in their bright summer clothes ran around excitedly. Molly was keeping an eye on Luke and Lily so that Stuart and Anna could mingle and talk. She could see them now, Stuart introducing someone to Anna. Molly felt pleased that they were getting to know people and becoming part of the community.

Inwardly though, she felt an ache of sudden loneliness. It crept up on her sometimes, the reality that she was on her own. She took another sip of her drink, giving herself a mental shake. It was far too beautiful a day for such gloomy thoughts.

Glancing over she saw Lily and Luke had joined their parents so decided to wander into the marquee and was delighted when she spotted Judy. Looking very elegant with a pink silk scarf draped loosely over her shoulders, she was talking to a man.

Stuart had told Molly about the extension of the museum which showcased the university's collection of artefacts. The space was also going to be used for events such as workshops, theatrical and musical performances. Local businesses and donors had made generous contributions to make it possible so she guessed that was why Judy was there.

Judy caught her eye now and beckoned her over. Molly weaved her way through the tables of drinks and nibbles just as the man turned to leave. His gaze slid over Molly and he flashed her an easy smile as he passed.

'I hope I didn't interrupt you.' Molly smiled.

'Quite the opposite, you rescued me,' replied Judy.

'Oh? That doesn't sound too good.'

'That man you saw is Greg Ritchie. He owns a large hotel in St Andrews.'

'You were discussing business?'

'Not the kind of business he'd like to discuss.'

Molly didn't understand. 'Sorry?'

'After George passed away, Greg Ritchie came to see me after leaving what he obviously thought was a respectful amount of time. He wanted to know if I'd be interested in selling the inn.'

'How insensitive of him.'

'I don't think he's a bad person or anything. Just a businessman on the lookout for his next deal. He has plenty of charm on the outside but he's a hard-bitten business man. He gave me his spiel – how sorry he was, how running this business on my own would be difficult and he was prepared to make me a good offer. He keeps thinking I'll change my mind. And of course, it's typical of him to use an occasion like this.'

'That's terrible.'

'Oh, it's nothing I can't handle, I've met his type before. As flight attendants, we were trained to deal with difficult passengers – you simply try to deflect the situation. So that's what I did when I called you over – sorry, I hope you don't mind.'

'Not at all,' Molly replied, noticing the small frown creasing Judy's forehead. 'Try not to let him upset you.'

Judy gave a watery smile. 'I know. What does upset me is that every now and then I find myself thinking of how much more I should be doing with the business, as Greg Ritchie likes to point out. I say to myself, today I'm going to do this or that but then

I can't seem to find the energy. I suppose I've got into a bit of a rut.'

'That's understandable,' Molly sympathised.

'Things are ticking over nicely but I know I could do more. I'm more of a people person to be honest while George was the brains with all the ideas. The inn is busy enough but at times I feel as though I'm just limping along. George had so many plans and sometimes I feel as if I'm letting him down in some way.'

'I'm sure that's not the case at all.'

Judy gave a sad smile. 'I suppose there are times when I miss him more than usual, today being one of them.'

'What was George like?'

'Oh, he was very handsome and charming. He was what I suppose you would call old school. He'd been in the Royal Air Force where he trained as a pilot and served for fifteen years before becoming a commercial pilot. We used to meet on the occasional long-haul flight and then one day we were both delayed at Atlanta airport for a few hours. We got chatting and well, that was it really. We had a wonderful life together even though it wasn't long enough.'

It seemed sad and unfair that someone like Judy mourned and missed a love she once had while other people – namely Molly's ex-husband – discarded relationships as if they had meant nothing. At least Judy had known that real passionate love. Had she ever had that with Colin, Molly wondered. If so, surely they would still be together.

'It sounds like you had something very special.' Molly smiled. And George must have been a special man, she was sure, to still make Judy's face light up the way it did. Even his memory seemed to give her an inner glow.

'We did.' Judy took a drink, eyeing Molly over the rim of her glass. 'What about you?' she asked. 'Do you have someone special in your life?'

Up until recently, her wedding ring might have answered that question, thought Molly, suspecting a band of gold was something Judy would notice. Now she felt her bare fingers twist around each other as she answered.

'I'm actually divorced.' It felt strange saying it out loud.

'I'm so sorry to hear that. What a terrible thing to go through, a lovely young thing like you too. It happens to the best of us though.'

Molly gave her a grateful smile. 'But I'm loving being here with my brother and his family. I'm trying to see this as a new beginning,' she said brightly, determined to keep up her positive front.

'Not always easy though, is it?' Judy eyed her shrewdly. 'Tell me how you got on the other day. Did you go to the golf range?'

Molly pulled a face. 'I did but I was a bit rusty and having a hangover didn't exactly help. The night before was the first night of my holiday and I think I may have celebrated too much. But hopefully I'll improve while I'm here with some more practice.'

Judy chuckled. 'Did you meet Joe or Tom?'

'Um, I met Tom.'

'He's a bit lovely, isn't he? He and Joe are a couple of lovely lads. They're certainly breathing new life into that place. Joe's very much the frontman, always ready with a joke and having a laugh with people and Tom, well, he's quieter, more of a private person. He comes over now and again to have his evening meal or sometimes just for a chat. I must admit I've got a bit of a soft spot for him.'

Molly smiled blandly as visions of his body on the beach this morning flickered through her mind. She was beginning to suspect she might have several soft spots for Tom Kennedy. She cleared her throat. 'He told me about the junior tournament they're running.'

'Tom told me, it's a wonderful idea.'

A small crowd of people clutching their drinks passed by and Molly took a step back to let them by. She looked across to Judy, recognising something in her expression and wondered if it was loneliness. She certainly understood how easy it was to feel alone just as she had done a few moments ago – that feeling of being on the outside looking in. She felt a little wave of sympathy just as an idea struck her. 'How about we go for a game of golf one day?'

Judy's eyes opened wide in surprise.

'But I can't play at all. I've never even held a club before.'

'That's the whole point. You don't need lessons first, it's just a case of getting out there.'

Judy's stared into the distance, her eyes taking on a faraway look. 'George always did want me to play with him,' she sighed.

'Think how proud he would be of you,' Molly said gently.

'And you'd really want to play with me?' she asked doubtfully.

Molly nodded her head eagerly. 'We don't need to take it all seriously or keep score. It'll be fun, I promise. And we can have a good old natter.'

Judy's cheeks radiated a little blush of pleasure. 'In that case how can I refuse?'

# Chapter Six

The next morning Molly was woken by sounds from the garden. She yawned and then groaned, her unused muscles protesting from their run on the beach yesterday. Slowly, she rose from her bed and padded across the floor to the window where she could see Luke and Jamie, the little boy from next door, kicking a football about in the garden. She smiled, watching a little brown-and-white dog scampering around frantically trying to join in and wondered how long it would be before Luke started pleading for a dog of his own.

As she stood for a few moments gazing out she couldn't help comparing it to the view she was used to from her bedroom at home. Any greenery there had once been was now eclipsed by the never-ending sea of houses being built. Inspired by the beautiful morning Molly chose a pale blue sundress, making her feel summery and light, and headed downstairs where Anna and Lily were in the kitchen finishing their breakfast.

'You look nice today,' Anna commented. 'Did you sleep well?'

'I did, thanks.'

'There's some coffee left in the pot and I've kept a croissant warm if you'd like one,' Anna said.

Molly swallowed down a sudden lump in her throat at Anna's

thoughtfulness, all her recent solitary meals coming to her mind. Even before Colin left she could hardly remember the last time they'd shared breakfast – on weekdays he left too early and on weekend mornings he'd be at the gym. It felt as if the more time she spent here, the more Molly was able to look back at how lonely she'd become in her marriage. And while she loved Anna for it, she didn't want to get used to it. She had to face the reality of her future alone – for the foreseeable future anyway.

'Lovely thanks,' she said over-brightly, reaching for a cup. 'Are you remembering I'm making dinner tonight?'

As a special treat today Anna and Stuart were taking Lily and Luke on the train across the Forth rail bridge to Edinburgh – Luke was beside himself with excitement – so Molly had offered to prepare the meal for tonight.

'You're still happy to do that?' Anna checked.

'Of course. I'm looking forward to exploring the farmers' market.'

After breakfast and saying her goodbyes, Molly looped her bag over her body and set off. Closing the front door behind her, she smiled at the sight of the morning sun shimmering on the sea. To have that view all year and be able to see the fleeting changes depending on the light or the season must be wonderful.

There was a real buzz about the town, with holidaymakers and golf fans all making the most of the warm weather. Molly could feel the heat of the sun on her back and was grateful for some shade as she made her way through the narrow alleys and old wynds of the town, pausing every now and again to admire the elegant curves of the Georgian buildings.

The market was already in full swing when Molly arrived and soon she was milling about with the throng of people. She'd forgotten the delights of fresh produce and hardly knew where to start. Stalls were bursting with seasonal fruits and vegetables while others displayed homemade pickles, jams and organic bread.

Enticed by the delicious cooking smells, she paused for a few minutes to watch fresh scallops being prepared at a cookery demonstration and then tasted a sample of locally brewed craft beer.

She stopped at the cheese stall, spoilt for choice from the array of flavours. Tempted by the smoky garlic cheddar, creamy smooth Bries and crumbly blues, she finally decided on a cheese named Caboc, a soft cheese rolled in toasted oatmeal. Finally, she bought some fresh salmon, a large rustic loaf and a pile of vegetables. Happy with her purchases Molly became aware how hot and thirsty she had become.

She wondered how the train trip across the Firth of Forth was going, realising the guest house would be empty when she returned. Like breakfast this morning, she reflected how easily she'd got used to the noise and activity of the guest house, the signs of family life everywhere – shoes discarded in the hall, toys scattered in practically every room, swimming things hanging up to dry.

She told herself it would be good to have some time by herself, she'd be able to do some thinking and planning. This morning she'd received an update from the estate agent's in Glasgow letting her know there'd already been a few viewings, so she should really start to look at flats available for renting. Unlike West Sands, her former marital home would be sitting empty for the foreseeable future, the rooms lying silent. The image filled her with such sadness that it almost took her breath away. Suddenly and unexpectedly she felt tears looming and dug her nails into the palm of her hand, telling herself to get a grip.

A cool drink and some shade, that was all she needed. After purchasing a fruit juice at one of the stalls, she scanned her surroundings and spotted an area of grass away from the main thoroughfare with a couple of benches in the shade beneath a sycamore tree.

It was only as she drew closer that she saw Tom Kennedy occupying one of the benches, his long legs stretched out in front of him and his arms splayed along the back. A man always slightly apart from the crowd, she thought. But then she could understand that – after all, wasn't that what she was doing right now?

She headed towards the empty bench, pretty sure he wouldn't want company but he straightened up as he saw her and gestured to the seat beside him.

'I'm not disturbing you?' she checked.

'No. I'll need to go soon anyway.'

Perhaps not the most effusive greeting but still, she was grateful to be off her feet. Like every other time she had met him, he seemed capable of making her feel oddly unsettled, unsure whether he really wanted to talk to her or not.

She sat down, catching a hint of his woody, masculine after-shave before she took a sip of her drink. He inclined his head towards her bulging shopping bag at her feet. 'You've been to the market?'

'My turn to make dinner tonight.' She smiled. 'It's ages since I've been to a market. My shopping usually resembles a super-market sweep – grabbing a basket, then in and out as quickly as possible.'

He chuckled. 'Where is it you live?'

'Glasgow,' she replied. 'Do you know it at all?'

'Not well. I've visited plenty of cities but never lived in one. I'm not sure I could do it.' His eyes seemed to go somewhere else for a moment as he looked into the distance. 'I need open views and breathing space.'

Molly had lived in Glasgow her whole life. She liked the energy and vibrancy of the city and while perhaps she hadn't always necessarily taken advantage of everything on offer, she liked knowing it was there. Although these last few mornings she had found it very calming waking to the sea, almost as if she could breathe more easily.

'I can certainly see the attraction of living somewhere like here.'

60

'You'll be able to visit your brother and his family though, right?'

Molly nodded, the thought giving her comfort.

'How long are you staying here for?' he asked her.

'Um, I'm not sure, to be honest. I'm between jobs at the moment and so I'm not in any particular hurry.'

'I didn't see you on the beach this morning.'

'Ah no, I didn't quite make it today.' He didn't need to know she could hardly walk this morning let alone run. 'Not sure running is really my thing.'

'Stick to the golf?'

'Probably,' she laughed, feeling herself begin to relax. 'Although I should probably get some more practice in before my parents arrive. They're coming to watch some of the tournament but no doubt my dad will want to prove he can still beat me.'

'He's a keen golfer?'

'Both my parents play and they were lucky enough to take early retirement and now they live beside a beautiful course in Portugal.'

'Sounds idyllic.'

The town was so busy now with the build-up to the tournament, it was difficult to escape from it all and she wondered if Tom ever wished he was still part of it all.

'Do you ever miss being on the tour?'

There was a slight pause. 'I don't tend to think about it much.'

Molly imagined his previous life to be far removed from anything she knew and found herself interested. 'What was life like on tour?'

Tom run a hand along his jaw, hesitating for a moment. He spoke slowly at first, almost as if he was dragging the memories to the front of his mind. 'The early years were the toughest. It can be lonely travelling to obscure parts of Europe.' He gave a half-smile. 'I've stayed in some pretty dire hotels.'

'So it's not all glamour and glitz?' Molly gently teased.

Tom smiled wryly. 'Definitely not. But of course, the better you do, the easier it becomes. Then you get to play on amazing courses, stay in top hotels, get wined and dined…'

'If you don't do well enough you can lose your card that lets you play or get relegated to a lower tour, is that right?'

Tom raised his eyebrows, looking surprised by her knowledge. 'That's right. The pressure to do well is constant and it's very competitive. It can be difficult deciding when to give up. Joe and I became good friends on the tour and we used to discuss it sometimes. He was always interested in the coaching side of things and hadn't been playing his best golf so knew he was heading to the lower-ranked tournaments. He'd met Beth by then and after they married, I don't think his heart was in it anymore. They decided to settle here in St Andrews and Beth's actually expecting their first baby.'

'That's nice for them.' Molly smiled. She glanced at him with a curious look. 'So why did you give it up?'

She saw his shoulders stiffen slightly. 'I broke my leg in an accident – a hotel fire in Italy.' He spoke matter-of-factly, his tone deliberately neutral.

'Oh, I'm so sorry. That's terrible.'

'It was after then that Joe asked if I wanted to come in with him and run the golf school. So that's what I did – it was a great opportunity. I've been lucky.'

Molly wasn't an expert in body language but you'd have to be blind not to see he wasn't exactly comfortable with the topic. He stared at a spot on the ground looking thoughtful, a small muscle working in his jaw. He took a breath as he faced Molly, their eyes meeting for what felt a long moment.

'I was—' He started to speak just as two middle-aged men appeared from nowhere in front of them, greeting Tom like a long-lost friend.

At first Molly assumed they knew Tom but it soon became apparent they were golf fans looking for Tom to autograph the caps they were clutching. Molly thought there was something slightly comical about them, like they were overgrown excited schoolboys, but they were clearly golf fanatics intent on making the most of the moment.

Tom stood up and Molly watched him go through the motions. He was pleasant enough but his discomfort was obvious to her and she watched his fingers flexing as they asked him a few questions about the upcoming tournament.

Molly wasn't sure what happened but somehow the mood had shifted and she saw his eyes had become distant, like a shutter had come down.

Just as the two fans bumbled off with enthusiastic thanks and waves, a vision in white jeans and a halter-neck top complete with a mane of dark hair and to-die-for cheekbones appeared.

'There you are, Tom. Where have you been hiding?'

Molly furtively regarded the woman who was now placing a perfectly manicured hand on Tom's arm, feeling herself shrink in the face of such perfection. The woman threw a cool look in Molly's direction. 'I'm not interrupting anything, am I?'

'Er, no. Gemma this is Molly. She's staying at West Sands Guest House—'

'Nice to meet you.' She raised a hand dismissively. 'But we really should get going, Tom. I've got a good feeling about this house.'

Tom looked slightly uncomfortable before he glanced over at her with a resigned shrug. Molly found herself alone on the bench, something beginning to feel familiar about seeing Tom being led away by an attractive female. She finished her drink and had no idea why she suddenly felt so deflated.

**** 

A few hours later, Molly sat with a large glass of wine supervising Lily chopping peppers and tomatoes. Molly was pleased when Lily agreed to help prepare the meal tonight and was keeping a close eye on her to make sure there were no accidents. Lily appeared to relish being entrusted to cut up the vegetables that Molly had brought home and was taking her duties very seriously, her mouth set in a small line of concentration.

Molly took a sip of wine and then turned her attention back to her laptop. Her intention had been to look at some job vacancies but somehow she had ended up Googling Tom Kennedy. She told herself there was nothing stalker-ish about it. She didn't know quite why she was doing it – especially as he appeared to be involved with someone – but some strange compulsion had taken over her and she had to find out what had happened.

She found a few articles easily enough on the fire that had ripped through the top floors of the Palazzo Lacarno hotel in Rome last year on the last night of the European tour. One man had died and several others had been injured. Tom had been playing the best golf of his professional life and been poised to win the title before the fire had broken out.

By all accounts Tom had been a hero and had been involved in rescuing people which had resulted in him breaking his leg and subsequently giving up the tour. Although there were several articles and interviews, there wasn't a single comment or quote from Tom himself.

Molly thought back to earlier and how uneasy he had become with the golf fans and then recalled Judy telling her he was a private man. But there had also been that brief moment earlier when he had looked at her and she had felt a moment of connection. She felt like she was piecing together a complicated puzzle and was forming the impression that there was a lot going on beneath the surface with Tom Kennedy.

'What next, Aunt Molly?' Lily's voice broke into her reverie. Molly jumped, feeling rather guilty, and snapped the screen of the laptop closed. Putting down her glass, Molly stood up and joined Lily. 'That looks great, well done. Next we drizzle olive oil and then sprinkle some sea salt and black pepper.'

After opening a few cupboards to locate an oven tray, they tipped in all the vegetables and gave it a good mix. 'Now we can put it in the oven for around half an hour.'

Earlier Molly had marinated the salmon fillets with olive oil, lemon juice and parsley and they were wrapped in foil already in the oven.

'Will I set the table now?'

'Thanks, Lily, that would be great. And I'm sure Luke will help you, won't you, Luke?' She lifted an eyebrow looking down at Luke who had appeared crawling along the floor playing with his cars. He appeared to consider the request for a moment before his cheeks dimpled into a smile. 'All right.'

'Thanks, kids.' Molly nodded in satisfaction as they scuttle off to find plates and cutlery.

'Okay, what have you done to my children? They're setting the table and not fighting with each other.' Anna came into the kitchen, slapping down a pile of papers on the kitchen table.

'That's because you're their mum—'

'—whereas you're their cool aunt.' Anna grinned.

'What's that you've got there?' Molly asked.

Anna gave her a sheepish look. 'I've been approached about a job so I'm taking a look at the details.'

'I thought you were going to take a few weeks off?'

'I know, but I hate to turn work down.' Anna grimaced, helping herself to a glass of wine from the open bottle. 'I'm just taking a look.'

'What's the job?' Molly wiped her hands and joined her at the table.

'It's a Scottish company, they manufacture engineered structural timber. They're looking for a small freelance team to develop desktop applications – all stuff I've done before so it shouldn't be too demanding.'

Molly couldn't help wondering what Anna's definition of demanding was.

'I'd probably need to go to Forres now and again,' Anna continued.

'Forres. That's up north, right?'

'About a four-hour drive from here or I suppose I could get the train,' she murmured almost to herself.

'But you don't have to do it,' Molly suggested lightly.

'No.' She shrugged. 'But I've never turned down a job before.'

Molly knew how much Anna's career meant to her and could understand it being difficult for her to turn work down. But she worried that her sister-in-law was pushing herself and was sure a proper break would do her the world of good.

Anna pushed the papers to one side and Molly hoped that Anna didn't feel pressurised into taking the job. Just then they heard the front door followed by a chorus of 'Daddy!' as Luke and Lily scampered through to the hall to greet him. The two women shared a smile and as she went to serve dinner, Molly thought to herself what a lovely way that was to be welcomed home.

66

# Chapter Seven

A few mornings later Molly walked into the kitchen where a stand-off between Luke and Lily appeared to be in progress. They were scowling at each other, Lily standing guard in front of the fridge with her arms crossed and her mouth set in a tight line.

'Hello, you two,' Molly said brightly, hoping to diffuse the impasse. She soon discovered the dispute was over breakfast.

'Luke wants ice cream for breakfast just 'cos Mum isn't here,' Lily informed Molly, keeping her eyes fixed on her little brother.

'She's not the boss of me.'

'Yes I am, I'm the oldest.'

Luke was wearing his Spiderman pyjama top over his trousers – not necessarily unheard of but combined with his un-brushed hair and odd socks, Molly was fairly certain he'd dressed himself. Lily's dark hair was pulled into a messy ponytail and Molly's heart lurched at how young and vulnerable they looked.

'Where is everyone?' she asked, looking from one to the other.

'Dad had to go to work for a meeting and he told us to get dressed by ourselves and have breakfast. He said to leave Mummy in bed because she's got a sore head. And he put me in charge.' Lily lifted large eyes to Molly, and her earnest expression reminded her so much of Stuart when they used to argue as children.

Molly chewed her lip thinking. That didn't sound like Anna at all. She realised two pairs of eyes were now regarding her solemnly, awaiting her adjudication. She racked her brain trying to think of a way of sorting this without upsetting either of them and hopefully remain their favourite aunt.

'How about we have some cereal and toast now and then as a treat, I'll take you for a really special ice cream later?'

Luke's approval was immediate and he happily took a seat at the table and was already reaching for the cereal box as Molly raised questioning eyebrows to Lily. Molly felt her shoulders sag in relief when she was rewarded with a conciliatory shrug as she joined her brother at the table.

'You two start and I'll just pop up to see your mum, okay?'

Upstairs, Molly knocked gently on Anna's bedroom door and crept into the room. The blind was half open so she was able to make out Anna's silhouette on the bed. Molly blinked as her eyes adjusted to the darkness.

'Anna?' she whispered.

'I'm just getting up.' Very slowly, she sat herself up, her eyes narrowing in pain against the sliver of light from the window.

'Don't move,' Molly urged. Usually so full of energy, it felt terrible to see Anna like this. 'Do you need to see a doctor?'

'No, I'm fine,' she croaked, looking anything but fine. 'It's just a migraine – I haven't had one for a long time but I always keep medicine to take in case. I just need to lie in the dark for a while.' She managed a weak smile but looked utterly exhausted.

'Can I get you anything?'

Anna gently shook her head. 'Stuart won't be long, he only had to go in for a meeting this morning. It's just the children—'

'I'll take care of them,' Molly said fluffing up the pillows so Anna could lie down again. 'You stay here and don't worry about anything. I'll have my phone if you need anything, okay?'

Back downstairs and with bowls of cereal consumed and dishes washed and put away, Molly turned her attention to the day and what to do. She was sure she'd read an article recently saying that boredom was good for kids' creativity but didn't necessarily want to test that theory today. She needed to get them out of the house, but suddenly the day stretching ahead of them seemed quite long. The sun was out so that was promising.

'Would you like to go to the beach?'

'No,' came the unanimous reply. At least they were agreeing on something, thought Molly optimistically.

'Can we go to the aquarium again?' Luke suggested brightly.

'Uh-uh.' Lily shook her head.

Spotting her golf clubs in the hall, inspiration came to Molly. She remembered the junior tournament Tom had mentioned and didn't know why she hadn't thought of it before – the golf range would be perfect for the children.

'Kids, how'd you like to go to the golf range?'

'Yay!' Luke jumped up and down excitedly.

'Great, that's decided then,' Molly said, taking Lily's resigned shrug as agreement.

An hour later Molly almost regretted her suggestion to take a picnic, such was the time it took to organise with more disputes over what fillings to have for the sandwiches. It took much longer to get ready than Molly ever could have imagined – getting dressed and finding shoes, brushing teeth and applying sun cream. The process renewing Molly's respect for parents everywhere.

Eventually, they were all bundled into the car and ready to go. They drove along the coastal road with the sea sparkling beside them. The children fell quiet in the back of the car and Molly spied Lily from her rear-view mirror staring out of the window. She wondered what she was going through her mind and hoped she wasn't worrying about her mother.

Molly's previous visits to Drumloch had been by foot but this time she drove along the main road before turning into another short stretch of road which brought her to the small car park in front of the golf school. As she brought the car to a stop, Molly looked around, always struck by the sense of tranquillity and beauty of the location.

Lily and Luke were already scrambling out of the car as Molly rummaged in her bag for her sunglasses. Climbing out of the car, she spotted Tom right away in one of the teaching bays with an older man in the middle of a lesson. Luke happily skipped ahead while Lily trailed behind, seemingly not yet fully convinced this was a good idea. As she drew closer Tom looked over and gave her a small smile, making Molly glad she'd washed her hair this morning and chosen to wear the pretty cream lace top with her denim skirt.

With the help of Kenny in the reception area, they were soon sorted with buckets of balls and suitable clubs. Molly thought it best just to let Lily and Luke get used to holding the clubs and have a go at hitting the balls. Without a shred of self-consciousness, Luke began to whack the balls, not even waiting to see where one landed before hitting the next one. Lily on the other hand was more considered and took her time lining up each ball and watching to see how far she had hit it. Molly wanted to make sure they didn't think there was a right or wrong way, she just wanted them to enjoy it.

'That's it, well done,' she encouraged Luke while surreptitiously glancing over at Tom. The lesson appeared to be finished now and he was chatting to the man. Even from a distance Molly felt acutely aware of his physical closeness. She didn't know what it was about him that affected her so much. She wasn't sure how to process it, except to know it wouldn't do her any good.

'Like this, Aunt Molly?'

Giving her head a little shake, she turned her attention to Luke. Mustering all his might, he thwacked the ball as hard as he could, shouting in delight as the ball shot into the air and reached the fifty-yard marker. Molly spent the next few minutes watching Luke and Lily. She was delighted to see them having fun and more than a little relieved. Hopefully with all this energy being expended there'd be less chance of fractiousness later.

Seeing their buckets of balls were nearly empty and realising their time was almost up, Molly went to fetch the picnic bag from the car.

When she returned a couple of minutes later, the man who had been with Tom was talking to the children. He was tall, with snowy white hair and twinkly grey eyes and judging by the way he had Lily and Luke giggling, Molly had more than a sneaking suspicion he had grandchildren of his own.

He introduced himself as Harry, joking that the children were playing better than him after his sixth lesson. After a while Tom came over and Harry bid the little group farewell.

'You look as if you have your hands full today.' Tom smiled, nodding his head towards the children.

Molly glanced at him, suddenly feeling shy and self-conscious. She'd thought about him often – probably too often – in the last few days and seeing him again now, she felt her body reacting to him. She took a breath, trying to calm herself, and turned to introduce Luke and Lily.

'Hi, guys.' Tom grinned at them. 'How are you getting on? Are you enjoying yourselves?'

'I'm really rubbish,' Luke informed him happily.

'Not at all, I was the exact same at your age. You just have to keep practising.'

Much to the children's delight, Tom fetched another bucket of balls and then spent the next half hour helping them to take shots. Molly stood watching, her heart lifting to see Lily so clearly enjoying herself.

Tom hunkered down so he was eye to eye with Luke and helped him line up his next shot. Her eyes drifted to Tom's forearms and Molly thought she might be slightly obsessed with them.

Watching as Tom now helped Lily take a shot, Molly appreciated how patient and encouraging he was while also making it fun. 'Will I be as good as you one day?' Luke asked Tom earnestly.

'You'll be better than me if you practise and work hard,' Tom assured him.

'Can you get rich playing golf?' Lily asked, sounding so serious that Molly had to bite her lip not to laugh.

Tom let out a low chuckle. 'Well, top players can.'

'Are you a top player?'

'Not anymore,' he said with a half-smile. 'Now I'm happy to teach golf.'

'Talking of which,' Molly interjected, 'I think we've taken up enough of your time today.' She raised her eyebrows at the children. 'What do you say to Tom?'

'Thank you,' they chorused.

'They really enjoyed that, thanks.' Molly smiled, appreciating he had given them what was basically a free lesson.

'Molly, I'm really thirsty now,' Luke moaned, tugging at her sleeve.

'I can get you a glass of water from the office,' Tom offered.

Molly shook her head, holding up the picnic bag. 'We've actually brought our own.'

'You've come well prepared.'

'Have you ever thought about a drinks machine or even a café in the reception area?'

Tom looked a bit sheepish. 'Ah, yes. We've still got a long way to go. This is our first summer so we're not fully set up the way we want to be yet.'

Molly looked down, blushing. 'Sorry, I hope you don't think I'm being rude, telling you how to run your business. Only I've been in enough places with these two to know the usefulness of having a place for refreshments.'

'You're absolutely right. The reception area is something we need to develop – drinks are a priority.' He nodded solemnly but his eyes caught hers with a sparkle of warmth.

'We're having a picnic,' Luke announced.

'That sounds good.'

'We've got ham sandwiches.'

'And cheese and tomato,' Lily quipped.

'Right kids, let's go.' Molly started to head to the picnic area, pretty sure Tom wasn't interested in sandwich fillings.

'You know where the picnic area is?' he checked with her.

Molly nodded. 'The first day I came to the range, I went to the Drumloch Inn first. Well, I stumbled on it really,' Molly explained.

'So you met Judy?' He smiled affectionately.

Molly nodded. 'Yes, she's lovely. It was Judy who directed me to the golf school.'

'Well, I'm glad she did.' His gaze met hers and Molly's stomach did a strange little somersault.

'Can you come with us?' Luke suddenly interjected, looking up at Tom.

Molly shook her head at her nephew. 'I'm sure Tom's too busy to come with us.'

'Actually Harry was my last lesson for a while. I could take a break – that is, if you don't mind?' He looked at her questioningly.

'Of course, that's fine.' She shrugged nonchalantly, hoping she sounded more casual than she was feeling.

Tom disappeared for a minute to tell Kenny where he was going, leaving Molly to wonder why their unexpected lunch guest was causing her to feel quite so flustered. And watching as he strode back towards them, her eyes scanning his broad shoulders then lowering to his long, muscular legs, did nothing to make her feel less flustered. They fell into step as Lily and Luke ran on ahead.

'Harry seems a lovely man,' Molly commented.

'He's a real gentleman.' Tom smiled. He explained Harry was a widower and it came as no surprise to Molly to find he was the proud grandfather of two girls who he clearly doted on.

'Thanks again for spending time with Lily and Luke.'

Tom waved a hand, indicating it was nothing. 'I enjoyed it. I probably shouldn't admit it, but sometimes I actually prefer teaching juniors. Adults tend to spend hours obsessing about their swing whereas kids turn up with a total open mind. It might be easier if adults did the same,' he finished ruefully.

'Sometimes a bit of ignorance really is bliss?' Molly laughed, thinking how true his words were, not just with golf but most things in life.

Lily and Luke had reached a bench where Moly had already unzipped the cool bag and unpacked the food, laying it out neatly on the table.

'Thanks, Lily,' Molly said, taking a seat and reaching for the drinks. 'Is orange juice okay for you?' she asked Tom, holding up a bottle.

'Perfect, thanks,' he replied, taking it from her.

They all tucked in, chatting easily as they did. Molly and Tom shared a smile watching the children munching hungrily on their sandwiches and tearing open packets of crisps as if they hadn't seen food for days.

Once Luke and Lily had finished their food, Molly took out the Frisbee she'd remembered to bring and, with their energy replenished, she watched as Lily and Luke went off to explore their surroundings after shouting a warning not to go too far. She turned back to Tom, his legs now stretched out in front of him as he sat on the bench.

'All this greenery and countryside is a bit of a novelty for them.'

'Where were they living before?'

Molly filled Tom in about the family's move from Manchester as she cleared away some of the picnic debris and then sat back down. She smoothed down her skirt, their bodies suddenly feeling very close together.

She certainly hadn't expected him to join them but decided she was glad he had. He seemed quite relaxed – certainly more so than the last time they met after the market. She found herself wondering how his house hunting went.

'Um, how did your viewing go the other day?'

He frowned. 'It was a bit of a modern monstrosity actually, with a monstrous price tag to match – not really my thing.'

'Gemma seemed quite excited about it,' she said casually.

He nodded vaguely. 'You know what estate agents are like, they'll say anything.'

'Oh, she's an estate agent!' Tom looked at her questioningly and she realised she had perhaps sounded a bit too effusive.

'I thought…'

He raised an eyebrow. 'You thought?'

'That you and her, you know…'

'Me and Gemma? Definitely not.' He shook his head, looking slightly baffled. 'Although all the estate agents here have been very enthusiastic I have to say.'

Molly got the distinct impression that Tom Kennedy had caused quite a stir among the local estate agents although she wasn't sure he was aware of it.

He looked at her thoughtfully. 'Although I will probably go and see Willow Cottage again – I just haven't got round to it yet.'

'I think that's a great idea,' she said, not sure why that pleased her so much.

'Aunt Molly, catch!' Molly blinked, startled by the sound of Luke's voice. She turned just in time to see the Frisbee heading straight for her. Only Tom's quick reflexes prevented it from smacking her in the face. She placed her hand on her chest, laughing. 'That could have been painful. Thanks.'

Tom threw the Frisbee with ease back to Luke. As he sat back down, Molly noticed his hand grip the bench to ease the weight from the thigh as he sat.

'Does your leg hurt much now?' she asked gently.

'Some days it can be painful, it just depends. But I can control it with painkillers if I have to.'

'Was it difficult – the recuperation?' she asked, desperately hoping she wasn't over-stepping some mark.

'I was in hospital for a week and then I moved back in with my mother for several weeks while I recuperated.'

'What was that like?'

He gave a rueful look. 'Strange. My two sisters still live nearby so between them and my mum I was pretty well fussed over. But after a while, it was difficult not being able to do much – crime paperbacks and boxsets accounted for more hours than I care to remember.' He shook his head at the memory.

Molly thought it must have been a particular form of hell to go from being at your physical peak to lying around doing nothing all day. She watched as he absent-mindedly rubbed his hand along his thigh as he continued.

'It's been a long process to get to this point. After hospital I had weeks of physiotherapy, then hours of exercise – swimming, stationary bike, squats – to build up the weakened muscles and get my stamina back.' He gave his head a little shake. 'It's been frustrating at times but I'm getting there. And I keep pretty fit anyway and do plenty of exercises to strengthen the muscles which helps.'

'You certainly look fit anyway.' She bit her lip, had she really just said that? 'I mean, from a physiological perspective,' she clarified.

Tom just lifted his eyebrows at her and she looked down, suddenly feeling a bit hot and bothered until thankfully Tom changed the subject.

'So, how did you get into golf?' he asked her.

'It was my dad mostly who encouraged me. He'd take me and my brother to play although Stuart was never that interested whereas I loved it. My dad was always patient, even when I hit some terrible shots. I remember one hole on our local course where you had to hit the ball over a pond and time after time I'd lobbed the ball into the water. But he never got fed up with me. We must have got through a lot of golf balls!' She laughed now at the memory.

Realising she couldn't see the children, Molly stood up, shielding her eyes with her hand, and scanned the distance until she saw them. She waved over to them and sat back down.

'What about you, how did you get into golf? Was it your dad?' she asked him now.

'No, he died when I was thirteen.'

'I'm sorry, that must have been a difficult time.'

Tom nodded slowly. 'It was, I guess. More so for my mum. I have two older sisters so she had to bring us up alone after that.' He stared at the bottle in his hand as he thought back to those times.

'I don't think I made life easy for my mum for a while,' he admitted. 'My father had very much been the man of the house and with him gone I think I went off the rails for a while. I started to muck about at school, staying out late, drinking, that sort of thing. It was my grandfather – my mum's dad – who took me in hand and got me into golf which I think was my saving.'

'Where did you grow up?'

'A small village in the Highlands called Dornoch. I started to play at the local course. I suppose I had a natural talent for it and soon I was spending all my time at the golf range, practising for hours. My grandad was big on the etiquette and rules of the game. He'd always tell me golf was an honourable game – respect and concern for others – and he taught me that's how I should act in everyday life.'

'Sounds like a good man.'

'Yeah, he was. Anyway, I started winning titles and playing in national events. I turned professional when I was twenty-five and started playing on the tour.'

He continued with a small smile. 'I was lucky to be given the chance to play and I know the difference it made to my life. That's why I'd love to see more children – including girls – get the chance to experience it.'

Molly agreed. 'I'm so glad my father didn't dismiss the idea of me playing just because I was a girl. It's been such a big thing in his life and of course now he's retired he plays almost every day.'

77

Thanks to her dad Molly was more than able to hold her own in a conversation about golf and for a while they talked handicaps and birdies.

As they sat there under the canopy of trees with the dappled sunshine falling through the leaves, Molly thought it felt such a perfect moment. It was nice being able to sit and talk to Tom, like friends would do. It was just sometimes the way he looked at her and the way it made her feel – that's when it got a bit more complicated.

The peace was suddenly punctuated by Tom's phone buzzing. He looked down, swiping his thumb over the screen and Molly saw his brow crease into a frown.

'Excuse me a minute.'

As he took a few paces away from the table Molly waved over to Lily and Luke, indicating it was time to come back. As she finished tidying up, Tom returned, tucking the phone back into his pocket, a look of concern on his face.

'Is everything all right?' she asked.

He ran a hand over the back of his head. 'I think so, at least I hope so. Joe's wife has been taken into hospital.'

Molly listened carefully as Tom recounted what Joe had told him. 'Hyperemesis gravidarum – or morning sickness to you and me. Apparently though, this is nothing like ordinary morning sickness. There's a danger she could become dehydrated which can cause problems so she's on a drip and been given an injection to stop her being sick.'

'I know that can be potentially very serious,' Molly sympathised. 'But it sounds like she's been taken good care of.'

Tom looked thoughtful. 'She's going to be in hospital for a while apparently. I'll have to rearrange a few things at the school. I can cover most of the lessons and Kenny will be able to help out.' He spoke quietly, almost to himself.

Luke and Lily bounded up, looking happy and tired. Molly realised it was time to go and together they all headed back through the trees.

# Chapter Eight

The only good thing to come from Anna's prolonged migraine attack was Molly being able to spend proper time with Lily and Luke. She'd been slightly anxious at first, concerned how she would keep them entertained. It was one thing being the aunt who saw them a few times a year, swooping in for happy occasions with presents and giving them sneaky sweets and treats – it was quite another being responsible for their well-being for three days.

As things turned out, she needn't have worried. A selection of films thoughtfully provided at the guest house included the whole Harry Potter series and they'd enjoyed a couple of evenings curled up on the sofa with popcorn. They played a game of Monopoly that didn't seem to have any rules and had lasted the whole afternoon, and they'd spent a lovely afternoon on the beach, enjoying the simple pleasures of paddling and building sandcastles. As Molly sat eating an enormous ice cream in her bare feet with her jeans rolled up, she found herself picturing Colin with his new woman lounging in some luxury resort. She imagined her rubbing sun lotion into his back the way she used to do and was surprised when the image didn't upset her. Instead she bit into her ice cream cone, knowing she'd much rather be here.

Anna had stayed mostly in her room for three days. Molly was shocked at how debilitating the migraine was and did everything she could to help, taking her cold compresses, hot drinks and a few small meals. Her illness had coincided with a two-day seminar Stuart had been invited to – something to do with Scottish Medievalists – and he'd been all set to cancel but Molly insisted he go and that she could handle everything. She'd been happy to help and had been quite pleased with herself that she had taken care of the children without any major disasters or mishaps.

Anna was up and about and feeling better now, and although Molly thought she still looked tired and pale, she was keen to go on a viewing that had been arranged for today. Entering the kitchen, Molly saw Anna at the dining room table, hunched over what looked suspiciously like work documents. Not wanting to disturb her she quietly flitted about, boiling the kettle and finding teabags and then took the tea through. She placed a mug down beside Anna.

'Thought you might like a cuppa.'

'You're an angel, thanks,' Anna replied stretching out her back.

'What have you got there?' Molly asked peering over her shoulder before taking a seat.

'It's the contract for that job I told you about. I'm just taking a look through it, to see exactly what they want me to do.'

'Are you sure you should be doing that so soon?' Molly asked lightly just as Stuart strolled into the room.

'That's exactly what I said to her.'

'I haven't signed anything yet.' Anna replied, sounding tetchy.

'I thought we agreed you need a proper break. You said you weren't going to take on any more work.' Stuart gave his head a little shake, sounding mildly exasperated. While the little exchange hardly constituted an argument, for Anna and Stuart – who she'd never heard exchange a cross word – it was enough for Molly to feel a prickle of unease. Luke's bellowing voice broke into the silence that had descended on the room.

'I'll go,' Stuart said in a flat voice before leaving the room.

Molly put her mug down carefully on the table. 'Listen, why don't you go out, just the two of you?'

'Oh, Molly, that's kind of you but you've done more than enough these last few days.'

'But you've not been well, that's not the same,' Molly pointed out. 'You need some time alone. Please, Anna, I insist. And anyway, the kids and I have still got the last *Harry Potter* left to watch.'

Anna held up her hands. 'Okay, I'll think about it.

****

An hour later Molly and Anna were standing in front of a rather imposing, three-storey Georgian townhouse in the centre of St Andrews.

This time it was the owners themselves who opened the front door to the house. The couple introduced themselves and ushered them in as though Anna and Molly were old friends rather than viewers and their love for the house soon became apparent. They explained that as their family had all grown and left, they were now off to have an adventure of their own and had bought a cottage in the South of France. It had been a difficult decision for them to make – the house was much loved and filled with so many memories – but they were keen to sell up as quickly as possible so they could spend as much time as they could in France this summer.

The layout of the house was quirky. The ground floor consisted of two bedrooms and a bathroom with a sweeping staircase leading to the main living area on the first floor. At the top of the house, and with amazing views over the town and out to the sea, were a further four bedrooms, two of them en-suite.

Anna listened with rapt attention to the history of the house which had been built in the 1700s for a merchant family. Such was the couple's obvious affection for the house, Molly got the impression it mattered to them who bought it. They had spent years lovingly making it their family home and she could understand there would be a sadness in letting it go. But with so many rooms it also became apparent the house required a certain amount of upkeep and the lady said they were now looking forward to swapping house maintenance for the delights of their small cottage on the Cote d'Azur.

The couple left Anna and Molly alone and one look at Anna's face told Molly she was entranced, as they stood at the window of the master bedroom overlooking the garden. 'See? A south facing garden. That means we would get sun all day,' Anna enthused.

Molly smiled. 'So you like it?'

'I think it might just be perfect. It's close to the university which would obviously be ideal for Stuart and the children's school is only a fifteen-minute walk. Just think, no more one-hour commutes to school,' she sighed happily.

'So you think this might be the one?'

'Obviously I'll need to come back with Stuart but I think so. I really think this might be our forever house.'

The phrase 'forever house' repeated silently in Molly's mind. It sounded like the end of a fairy tale, the place you lived happily ever after in. Molly bit her lip, suddenly picturing herself moving out of her house and wondered where she would go.

She turned to Anna. 'I'm so happy for you,' she said, swallowing down the lump in her throat.

# Chapter Nine

The next morning Molly woke up bleary-eyed and unsettled. She'd spent the night tossing and turning and had finally fallen into a restless dream-filled sleep at some unearthly hour. Now her body felt heavy and reluctant to leave the cosy warmth of the bed. But hearing voices downstairs, she stretched out the weariness from her body and forced herself to move.

As had become her habit, she took a few steps over to the window to look out at the view. For the first time since she'd arrived, the sky was dark and overcast.

She didn't mean to pry but from where she stood at her bedroom window it was difficult not to glance into the neighbouring property where she could see Eva and Ben in their garden. Chickens were clucking and pecking at the seeds being scattered by Ben while Eva tended to the vegetables growing in a small patch at the bottom of the garden. In the middle of it Jamie kicked a ball around while their slightly manic-looking dog ran after him. Molly smiled at the idyllic scene. She saw Ben move over to where Eva was and gently place his hand on her stomach and then lean in to kiss the side of her face. Something about the gesture made Molly wonder if Eva was expecting a baby. There was something so loving and intimate about the moment, Molly had to turn away.

Anna and Eva had formed an instant friendship, bonding easily and quickly the way women with children often did. Anna had relayed Eva and Ben's story to Molly. She had been a widow living with her son Jamie running this house as a guest house. Ben had moved up from London to teach physics at the university and had moved in to the next-door house. They had fallen in love and were now married – and if Molly's suspicions were right, now expecting a child of their own.

Eva and Ben's story had filled Molly with hope on one level but fear on the other. What if she had missed her chance of happiness? She sighed heavily, tucking the thought away and turned from the window.

After showering and dressing Molly followed the sound of voices to the kitchen. Anna and Lily were singing along to a song on the radio as they tidied away the breakfast things while Luke, being held upside down and tickled by Stuart, let out a squeal of delight. For some reason the noise and jovial atmosphere jangled Molly's nerves. Perhaps she was more tired than she thought.

'Aunt Molly, we're going to see our new house today!'

'Wow, that's exciting,' she said, forcing herself to sound cheerful.

'We don't know if it's going to be our new house yet.' Lily had stopped singing and shot her brother a withering look.

'But Mummy likes it.'

'Did you like the house, Aunt Molly?' Lily asked her.

'I loved it…' Molly paused, feeling her phone vibrate, and, looking down, was surprised to see it was her estate agent calling from Glasgow. 'I'm just going to take this,' she said quickly, going to the hall. Answering it, Molly heard the chirpy tones of one of estate agents handling the sale of her house.

'We've got some great news for you. We've had so many view-ings and notes of interest in the house that we're putting a closing date for this Friday and we're expecting several offers.'

Molly blinked. That quick?

After listening to a few more details, Molly said goodbye, trying to get her head round the speed of the sale. She had guessed it would sell easily but hadn't been prepared for it to be so soon. That was good, she told herself, they had done a good job. This was what she wanted. She swallowed hard, not understanding why she was experiencing a tight knot in her stomach.

Anna, never one to miss a thing, looked at her when she re-entered the kitchen. 'Everything okay?'

'Um, sure. Just an update from the estate agent's. Looks like the house will be sold pretty soon,' she said brightly.

'It's all go on the house front for this family just now,' Stuart commented happily. 'You coming with us today, Molly?' he asked.

'Always glad to have you there,' Anna added. She had wasted no time in arranging a second viewing for the house today and although Molly appreciated being included, she thought it best they look at what could well be their new family home without her being there.

'Think I'll give it a miss if that's okay. There's a couple of shops I haven't had the chance to look at yet.' She gave a bright smile, ignoring Anna's look of concern.

Molly felt something stirring within her, a sense of unease, and was suddenly impatient for everyone to leave. She really needed to be by herself for a while. After what felt like an age, they finally left and Molly was on her own. Except now, in the silence of the house, she felt restless. She paced about, unsure what to do.

The beach, of course. A walk along the beach always helped put things in perspective and would help sort through the muddle of emotions welling up inside her.

A quick look out the window confirmed the sun was still in hiding so she grabbed her jacket and headed out. Taking a different direction today, she made her way to East Sands beach. She breathed deeply as she walked along the picturesque harbour, hearing the lap of water against the small fishing vessels bobbing in the water. She passed a little café, chalked lettering on a blackboard telling today's homemade soup was pea and courgette. Molly had no doubt it would taste delicious but her stomach churned at the thought of it right now. Inside she could see the café was bustling and it gave her a sudden, horrible feeling of being on the outside.

She reached the beach, which thankfully appeared empty of people, only a few squawking seagulls circling overhead. She trudged along and kept her head down, enjoying the feel of the sand beneath her feet. On and on she walked, trying to work out what she was feeling.

She thought of seeing Eva and Ben this morning and then her own brother and Anna. Everywhere she looked she was surrounded by happy families while what she'd had was broken. It felt as if her chances of having a loving family were slipping away. In a few days she'd be technically homeless as well as divorced and she suddenly felt very alone. Oh God, what a mess. Molly knew she was feeling sorry for herself but she couldn't help it. She tried to count her blessings, she really did but she wasn't able to prevent a cloud of isolation descending upon her.

It was also the shock of the phone call from the estate agent. As much as she didn't like the house, knowing it was to be sold this week felt so final. Her life with Colin really was over. She supposed she should probably let him know although she doubted he would be interested. She found herself wondering what he was doing right now, if he was truly happy. Did he have any regrets or had he really just flounced off without a backwards glance or thought for her. Had he thought so little of their marriage?

His betrayal suddenly came crashing into her. For the first time since she'd discovered his affair, Molly felt raw anger and pain at what Colin had done. It had been hidden underneath all that pretence of normality. But now everything seemed to hit her at once.

She stopped walking to look out at the horizon. Dark grey clouds hung heavily over the choppy water and the cool sea breeze stung her eyes. She stared out to the sea and stood motionless for a minute, a wave of misery building somewhere deep inside her. It started in the pit of her stomach, rose to her chest and then erupted in hot choking tears which spilled down her cheeks. The tears – which she'd been unable to shed before – were unstoppable. The brave face she had been putting on crumpled.

Her armour – the one she had painstakingly built since Colin left – had well and truly slipped. She felt shocked, as if she had only just found out her marriage was over. All she had ever wanted – a home and a loving family – wasn't going to happen. Perhaps she had sensed they didn't want the same things and had protected herself by not admitting to herself just how much she wanted those things. Now it was too late. She was on her own.

It was like grieving for something she would never have. She felt terrified and let down. A horrible hopelessness covered her. What was she going to do now?

Soon she was in full flow. Everything seemed to ache; her head, her eyes, her heart. Her body was racked by heaving sobs making her throat constrict. She had never cried like this before, didn't know she was capable of such a torrent of misery. As the waves of anger and hurt came crashing into her she knew she'd been holding herself in for a long time.

Feeling weak, she sat down. The sand was cool and damp underneath her but she didn't care. She gulped, trying to stem the flow of tears and took a deep breath.

She hugged her bent knees to her chest and stared out to the sea, keeping her focus on the ebb and flow of the water lapping against the shore until slowly, very slowly the tears began to subside.

She heard an uncomfortable cough from behind her. She

ignored it – whoever it was could go away. Then a deep voice asked if she was all right. She knew it was him before she looked up.

She turned swollen eyes to see Tom Kennedy looking at her, concern etched on his face. Given that she was sitting in the middle of a deserted beach with a tear-streaked face and looking like God only knows what, she didn't think there was much point in pretending.

'Not really.'

He didn't say anything, but sat down next to her. With his long legs stretched out before him, he followed her gaze out to sea.

'What are you doing here?' Instantly she regretted sounding so churlish. 'I just mean it's not exactly a day for the beach.'

'I could ask you the same thing.'

'Suppose.' She shrugged. 'I just needed to get away,' she said by way of explanation.

'Family holidays can be like that.'

'What?' She looked at him, frowning. 'Oh, no. It's nothing like that. It's...other stuff.'

'Anything you'd like to talk about?'

With absolutely not a single intention of telling him anything she took a breath and turned to face him. His blue eyes were fixed on her so intently and in that moment she was lost. She felt what was left of her defences crumble under the scrutiny of his gaze and the words simply tumbled out.

To her horror, she let out a sob. 'I want a forever house.' To her even greater horror, another round of tears began.

'A forever house?' He sounded slightly baffled.

'You know, the house you live in happily for a long, long time with the people you love.'

'Oh, right.'

'Except now I might never get the chance to have that,' she said flatly. She bent her head, picking at a shell embedded in the sand. The need to speak suddenly felt overpowering, almost physical. She had been desperate not to burden Stuart and Anna, determined to hold it all together. But the words, bottled up within her, needed to be unleashed. 'I...I got divorced a few weeks ago.'

'I'm sorry to hear that.'

She exhaled. 'And I just found out our house is to be sold this week.'

'And that was your – um, forever house?'

'No – I didn't even like it,' she told him shaking her head. 'I suppose it just makes everything feel real, it's really happened.'

Padding her pockets uselessly for a tissue, Molly resorted to a loud and rather inelegant sniff.

'How long were you married?'

'Almost five years.'

He paused and then spoke gently. 'What happened? I mean, you don't have to tell me.'

Molly hesitated for a second, aware she was telling him much more than he probably needed or wanted to know. But now she'd started, she didn't seem to be capable of stopping.

'I found out he was having an affair.'

'I'm sorry, that must have been tough.'

'It was,' she sniffed. 'But the thing is...I'm not sure how well things were going with the marriage anyway. It ended when I found out about his affair but I think Colin had left the marriage long before then.'

'What do you mean?'

Molly thought back to the small cracks that had started to appear in their relationship, a vague sense of them growing apart, two people together yet somehow separate. And she realised, it all revolved around his career.

'Colin worked for a financial company and worked hard. He always seemed to be getting promoted, earning lots of money which was important to him. And he enjoyed the trappings of his success but he liked them to be obvious, for all to see.' She waved a hand vaguely in the air. 'The fancy holidays, the expensive car, the exclusive gym membership. They were all that seemed to matter to him.'

Molly realised there was a point where perhaps she could have changed to what Colin wanted. But she knew she could never be that person. She shook her head sadly. 'I – I don't think I recognised him anymore as the man I married.'

'People change and not always for the better. Maybe it's as well to find out sooner rather than later.'

'I suppose,' Molly agreed before continuing. 'I knew I no longer fitted in with what he wanted – my job, my clothes, even the car I drove. I think he wanted this polished, manicured, high-achieving wife. I felt like I was constantly trying to do and say the right thing. Now I can see how awful that was.' She shook her head almost in disbelief.

'It's hard trying to be something you're not.'

Molly turned hearing the slight edge to Tom's voice. Staring into the distance, his eyes hardened for a fleeting moment before he blinked, pulling his gaze back to Molly.

'You must have had some good times though?'

'At the beginning, yes.' Molly stared down at her fingers, thinking. And as they continued to sit on the empty beach, Molly talked. It felt slightly surreal but she found herself telling Tom how she'd married Colin after university, how they'd bought the house on the outskirts of Glasgow. How everything seemed to be okay until Colin's promotion and then the marriage slowly started to fall apart. And how she was using this time to decide what came next. She wasn't quite sure how it happened but she found herself telling him things she hadn't told anyone else.

Perhaps it was his voice gently coaxing things from her or perhaps it was because he was looking at her with what appeared to be genuine concern. Either that or he was making a very good job of pretending.

'I guess I've been putting on a brave face and it all came tumbling down now. The thing is, I thought I was doing okay. Managing, you know. Up until about an hour ago and it all started to unravel.' She gave him a rueful smile. 'And I'm afraid you were in the wrong place at the wrong time.'

'Or the right place at the right time,' he countered.

Molly wasn't sure how to respond to that except she knew it made her feel a whole lot better for some reason.

A distant sound made them look up and Molly blinked in surprise to see a horse galloping along the beach. They sat and watched, something hypnotic and beautiful about the power and rhythm of the rider and horse as they galloped along the water's edge.

The unexpectedness of it seemed to bring Molly to her senses, pulling her back to reality. The reality being that she was sitting on a beach pouring her heart out to Tom Kennedy. She lifted her eyes to him, suddenly so aware of him. He really did have the most mesmerising, blue eyes and when they turned on you the effect was quite devastating. She suddenly felt self-conscious and attempted to smooth down her hair, hoping she didn't look quite as bedraggled as she felt. She was pretty sure Tom had somewhere to go, somebody to be with.

'Anyway, um, thanks for listening. And I'm sorry. I'm sure you didn't need to hear all this.'

'You don't need to apologise. Sounds like you've had a rough time.'

She sat up inhaling the air, noticing she did feel better, like a weight had been lifted. 'Are you sure you're not some sort of therapist as well as a golfer?' she joked feebly.

He let out a low chuckle. 'No but I know plenty of people who use the golf course as a way of escaping things in life.'

A sudden cool breeze had picked up and Molly realised she could no longer feel her fingers and her backside was frozen. She shivered and felt Tom's gaze on her.

'Listen, how about we move from here. Go for a walk or maybe get a drink to warm you up?'

'That's all right. I'm fine now, honestly.' She hated that he might feel obliged but his gaze remained focused on her.

'I'm not leaving you here,' he stated.

She looked at him through her lashes. 'Don't you have somewhere you need to be?'

'Nothing that can't wait. Come on,' Tom said, starting to move. He held his hand out to help her up and as Molly placed her hand in his, the touch of his skin sending a jolt of heat through her body. She suddenly became very focused on brushing sand from her jeans, giving her time to compose herself. They started to walk back towards the harbour, Tom pointing out various golf courses dotted along the coastline and a particularly noisy seagull made them laugh with a comical squawk. Molly looked up and saw some of the grey clouds had parted now, making way for glimpses of blue sky.

'How is Beth?' Molly asked suddenly, feeling terrible for not asking sooner.

'Still in hospital – they're keeping a close eye on her. Joe's spending as much time as he can with her.'

'What about the tournament?' Molly frowned, remembering it was in a couple of weeks.

His mouth tugged down at the corners. 'I might have to think about cancelling it. I mean, I don't want to but we're not organised for it properly.'

They had reached the café now that Molly had passed earlier and Tom suggested a hot drink. Molly, who was now chilled to the bone, didn't hesitate. The thought of something warm was simply too tempting.

Molly found a seat while Tom organised the drinks, bringing back mugs of tea to the table.

'Is this all right for you?' He looked at her with concern.

She nodded. 'I passed this place earlier and looked in, thinking how cosy it seemed.'

Molly warmed her hands on her mug, blowing gently on the steaming liquid before taking a sip.

'That's good, thanks,' she said gratefully, with a small smile.

She had only met him a few times and became conscious now of how much she had revealed to him today without really knowing much about him at all on a personal level. For all she knew, he might have someone special in his life.

'What about you – are you involved with anyone?' she asked tentatively.

'Not now.' He paused briefly. 'There was someone for a while. She worked as one of the physiotherapists on the tour. I had gone to her with a wrist injury and we started to see each other. Touring isn't always conducive to relationships so in that respect it worked well as we both understood the pressures of the lifestyle. It lasted a couple of years but ended after my accident. I had to focus on my recovery but Jen made it clear she didn't want to give up so she ended it.' He gave a small shrug. 'She liked her work and she liked the excitement of the tour. She's still with the tour as far as I know.'

Molly listened trying to picture Tom's life on the tour and found herself wondering about Jen. Tom's tone had been even, not giving much away and Molly couldn't work out if that was because it no longer mattered to him or because it was painful for him to talk about. She couldn't help wondering if he still had feelings for her and if they would have stayed together if Tom was still on the tour.

He looked across at her. 'How are you feeling now?'

'Better,' she replied truthfully.

'If you ever want to talk again you know where to find me.'

'Thanks.' His words gave her a warm, safe feeling inside. It was nice to know she could meet someone who seemed genuine, someone she might even become friends with. Because she knew that's all they could ever be, despite feeling drawn towards him. Molly knew that to trust someone again was going to be a monumental hurdle for her.

# Chapter Ten

'I can't believe how much I've enjoyed this!' Judy beamed.

'Didn't I tell you?' Molly replied happily. It had taken her and Judy just over two hours to complete the nine-hole course and now they were making their way to the last green.

'I'll be honest, I wasn't sure about playing golf. But it's actually been very relaxing,' Judy admitted.

Molly had managed to coax Judy onto the course, promising her it would be relaxed and informal with absolutely no score-keeping. Judy had dug out her husband's rather rickety trolley and old set of golf clubs.

'You'll think I'm a silly old fool but using George's clubs and trolley makes it feel like part of him is with me,' Judy had confided.

'I don't think that at all, I think it's lovely,' Molly told her. She was delighted that Judy seemed to have enjoyed herself so much. They had chatted about lots of things as they ambled their way round the course. Judy listened with interest as Molly described the work she'd been doing for the events company during the past year and aired some of her ideas about freelancing in the future. Judy obviously knew about Joe's wife being poorly and the possibility of the junior tournament being cancelled.

'That would be a terrible shame.' She had frowned, looking

thoughtful. 'Do you think it would be possible to help out in anyway?'

'I had been wondering about that too.' To Molly, the proximity of the inn to the golf course made them a natural partnership. The two businesses working together could be mutually beneficial and, as they continued round the course, Molly articulated some of the ideas that she realised had been bubbling around her head.

She inhaled deeply now, casting her eyes out to where the hazy blue sky met the glittering sea. She didn't think it possible to ever tire of that panorama. It lifted her spirits and made her feel anything was possible and she was filled with a sudden surge of energy and happiness.

It seemed her meltdown yesterday had done her the power of good. Bawling her eyes out in the middle of a beach had been quite cathartic and she hoped maybe she had turned some sort of corner. Now that she had faced up to how hurt she was, maybe she could start to move on.

Of course, she wouldn't have chosen Tom Kennedy to witness her breakdown but he had been understanding and she had felt surprisingly comfortable in his company.

She had seen a very gentle and caring side of him and snippets of their conversation from yesterday kept replaying in her mind. He had seen her in a vulnerable moment – her confidence was low and so was her trust in men for that matter. But the way he had looked at her and listened to her had made her grateful she had met him.

She didn't see any point lying to herself about the fact that she found him attractive but that was totally different from saying she wanted anything to develop between them. It would be easy to mistake physical attraction for something more meaningful. The time she had spent with him yesterday had almost felt like time away from the real world. Quite why she had confided in him she didn't know; looking back it was like she felt compelled to. Perhaps the old adage that it was easier to talk to a stranger was true except he didn't feel like one anymore.

After they'd left the café, he had insisted on walking Molly back to the guest house, checking several more times she was going to be all right. At the door he had gently caught her fingers in his, giving them a gentle squeeze.

'You know where to find me.' He had held her gaze, his voice low, and the way he had spoken, the way he had looked at her had left her feeling more than a bit flustered. She had to take a moment to compose herself before opening the front door.

In the house, she'd found Anna and Stuart sitting at the table, a bottle of wine between them and the decision made to put an offer in for the townhouse. Stuart and the kids had loved the house too and Anna's inheritance meant that they could make a good offer for it. Molly was excited and happy for them but after sharing a glass of wine with them, she had gone to her room early, feeling drained after all her emotional outpouring.

She'd done a lot of thinking in the last twenty-four hours and although the pain and hurt was still there, she didn't feel quite so hopeless. Very slowly she was putting her marriage with Colin in some sort of perspective. She realised she had swept so much of what she had been feeling away, ashamed her marriage had failed.

Looking back, she could see she had been lonely in her marriage, at least at the end of it. The hours Colin spent at the office – or so he claimed – meant they had been doing less and less together. Little by little Molly realised just how far apart they had grown. Molly almost felt a sense of relief that the affair at least explained what had been wrong. She had known something wasn't working and had been prepared to blame herself for it. With a jolt, she realised she had allowed Colin to think she was at fault in some way.

Slowly she was beginning to feel stronger and come to terms with everything.

Being here with her family was helping and she acknowledged that talking to Tom had helped.

They had brought their trollies to a stop at the last green now and Molly glanced at Judy. 'So do you think you would like to play again?'

'I think I would except I'd need a partner, wouldn't I? Maybe I should set up a singles golf club.'

'That's not a bad idea, you know,' Molly laughed. 'And you know golf is something you can actually get better at as you get older.'

'Well you certainly can't say that about many things in life,' Judy chuckled. 'And we've had a very good chat, haven't we?' They shared a conspiratorial smile before concentrating their efforts on the last hole, Judy taking several shots before hearing the satisfying plop of the ball land in the hole.

Molly had seen Tom earlier when she'd set off to play with Judy and she could see him again now with Harry, the widower she had met previously. They appeared to have just finished a lesson and were chatting outside the golf school as Molly and Judy approached.

After making introductions, Tom was keen to hear how their game of golf was. 'How did you enjoy it?' His eyes flicked to Molly and then Judy.

'We had a great game, didn't we, Judy?'

'It was wonderful. But I must admit I'm ready for a sit down now and a nice cool drink.' She rested her hand on her trolley at the precise moment the wheel – which had been wobbling throughout the game – finally gave way and fell off.

Judy stared down at it looking slightly aghast. 'Oh!'

Harry stepped up looking very gallant and smiled at Judy. 'Could I take that somewhere for you?' he asked.

'Oh, um, thank you. I don't have far to go, if you don't mind?' Judy said, managing to look suddenly very girlish as her cheeks flushed delicately.

Observing this little interchange, Molly watched Harry and Judy walking off together through the trees to the inn. She turned with a dreamy look on her face to find Tom looking at her, an eyebrow raised.

'What?' she asked innocently.

He gave his head a little shake.

'It would be nice, wouldn't it? Harry and Judy?' She smiled, watching them go off.

'I was going to make tea in the office, would you like one?'

She followed him through the reception area and into the back office. Molly looked around. There was a desk in the corner piled high with documents and scattered papers, several dirty mugs lying around and a sad-looking ivy plant wilting miserably on the window ledge.

'Excuse the mess,' Tom apologised with a sheepish grin. 'Joe and I aren't exactly on top of the paperwork just now.'

'That's understandable.'

Tom moved about the tiny kitchen locating tea things and Molly looked at some framed photos on the wall. They were of Tom and Joe, some formal ones taken during tournaments, others more casual where Tom looked happy and carefree. She smiled, the comradery between them obvious.

Tom looked over at her and grinned. 'Joe insists on putting them up.'

'You're good friends with Joe?'

'Yeah. The tour can be quite gruelling at times but we bunked up on countless nights in the same hotel room. Having someone you get on with makes it easier. Milk?'

'Please.'

Tom bent down to the fridge, his T-shirt riding just enough to reveal a few inches of perfectly toned skin. Molly swallowed hard and distracted herself by going over to the window.

The hills seemed to have been painted in a hundred shades of green and rolled into the distance. What an incredible view to have from your place of work, thought Molly, so very beautiful. More than could be said for the little ivy plant sitting in front of her which was looking decidedly saggy.

'Do you have anything to water the plant with – a watering can?' She gestured to the plant, turning to Tom.

'Er, no. I don't think it's ever actually been watered.' She tutted, rolling her eyes before finding a glass and filling it with water. Gently and gradually, she poured it in, watching as the dry hard compost thirstily soaked up the moisture. She took a step back and tilted her head, sure it looked perkier already.

She turned to find Tom watching her. His eyes sparkled and he flashed her a grin. 'Think we're missing a woman's touch round here.' He handed her a mug and the look he gave her sent a flash of heat through her body. 'Thanks,' she stuttered, clearing her throat. 'So, how is Joe's wife?'

'She's a bit better but she's still in hospital. I think they just need to keep a close eye on her but Joe's hoping she'll be out soon.'

Tom lifted his mug to his mouth, taking a drink. 'It's kind of strange to imagine Joe with a family. He's entering this whole new world I know nothing about.'

Molly nodded. 'I remember when my brother became a dad – he had a new role in life and it was kind of weird at first. I wondered how he was ever going to do it, but, of course, he did and he's a great dad.'

'I don't suppose anyone knows what it will really be like until they become a parent themselves.'

That was true, Molly mused. She had never taken the idea of becoming a parent for granted but she had hoped it was something she would be lucky enough to experience one day. A small sigh escaped and she became aware of Tom looking at her. 'You okay?'

She inhaled deeply. 'Of course,' she replied breezily, forcing her mind onto other matters, namely the tournament. 'So, er, have you thought any more about the tournament?' she asked.

He shook his head absently. 'We really don't want to cancel it. We don't want to let the children down. I'm going to see Joe tonight and we'll have a proper chat about it.'

'Judy and I were talking earlier and we thought it'd be a shame if you had to cancel. And well, we could help if you want.'

Tom's eyebrows shot up in surprise. 'Oh. I'm not sure what to say.' He came over to perch on the edge of the desk.

'In my last job I worked for an events company so I have a bit of experience. We organised everything from registration right through to the evening reception. Obviously the tournament is on a much smaller scale but the organisational principles are pretty much the same. The company's motto was "Fail to Prepare, Prepare to Fail". And I think the same stands true for your golf tournament…' Her voice trailed off, distracted by the way he was looking at her. She tucked a strand of her hair behind her ear and took a breath before continuing. 'Judy and I thought it made sense to tie up the facilities and came up with a few ideas.'

'O-kay,' he said, sounding doubtful. He ran a hand round the back of his neck. 'What did you have in mind?'

Molly chewed her lip, hoping her ideas would sound as good out now as they had earlier with Judy.

'Well, I can help with any administration easily enough. We could also generate a little bit of interest on social media – I can get Lily to help me with that. I reckon a lot of the children will have younger siblings – like Lily with Luke. So for the younger children I thought we could arrange a few activities – a putting contest, for example.

'We also thought a raffle would be a good idea. The prize could be dinner and a night at the inn for two followed by a game of golf the next day. Judy could also provide drinks for the adults during the event. The emphasis is very much on having fun but it also gives you an opportunity to showcase your facilities here.' She stopped speaking, feeling slightly breathless and aware she might have got carried away.

A grin flickered across Tom's face. 'You have been thinking about this, haven't you?' He paused with a small frown. 'Are you sure you'd want to get involved – aren't you supposed to be on holiday?'

'Honestly I'd love to help. Plus, you know, I'm sure I could cope with spending more time with you.' She smiled at him beneath her lashes.

'You could, do you?' A slow smile spread over his lips. 'Well, in that case, I'd really appreciate your help.'

'Great.' Molly beamed at him. He was looking at her thoughtfully.

'How about a game of golf? Would you like that?'

She looked at him doubtfully. 'I'm not really good enough to play with you.'

'Of course you are. And it'll be good for you to know the layout of the course before the tournament. We can take our time and there'll be no pressure.'

She looked down and then lifted her eyes to meet his. His smile was beautiful and stirred something deep inside her. She felt her mouth curve in response. 'Okay then.'

Still perched on the desk, he took her hand in his and gently pulled her towards him so she was standing in front of him. He drew her in closer just as Kenny clattered through the door carrying an assortment of clubs. With a quick mischievous smile, she stepped back letting her hand drop.

# Chapter Eleven

'Are you looking forward to your game of golf today?' Anna grinned at Molly.

'I am,' she replied truthfully. And madly nervous. She had exchanged numbers with Tom and when he'd texted to suggest today for their game, she'd agreed.

'Lily and Luke loved the golf range you know, they haven't stopped talking about it. The delectable Tom was quite the hit.'

'He was really good with them,' Molly agreed, draining the last of her tea. She checked the time and realised she needed to get going.

'I like your shorts – very snazzy,' Anna tittered.

'Oh God, do they look all right? They're not too short, are they?' Molly frowned looking down at the knee-length Bermuda shorts. 'I tried on about six outfits. It's a warm day but it might get cooler on the course and I want to be comfortable—'

'Molly, you look lovely, really you do. Stop fretting.'

Molly sighed, her shoulders sagging. 'Sorry, it's just the idea of playing with a professional making me jittery. Do you know how many people would love the opportunity to play with a pro?'

Anna gave her a knowing look. 'Mmm, and that's the only reason you're nervous?'

'Of course,' she said lightly, changing the subject. 'What about you? What are you up to today? Not sitting there too much longer I hope.'

'Don't worry about me. You've done more than enough these last few days. You go and enjoy yourself. It's been ages since you properly played golf, hasn't it?'

That was true. Apart from being nervous about playing with Tom, she was actually excited about playing again. She recalled all the times she'd asked Colin to play and he had refused. Now it felt good to be doing this. It wasn't just about the golf, it was about her doing something for herself.

An hour later, Molly drove up to the golf course and parked her car, her stomach a knot of apprehension. She retrieved her clubs and trolley from the back of her car and as she walked up to the golf school she saw Tom sorting through clubs, a cap pulled down over his eyes. He stopped what he was doing as she approached and took the cap off, running a hand through his hair.

'Morning.' He smiled.

'Good morning.'

'All set for the game?'

'I am.' She parked her golf trolley next to Tom's.

'But you will remember I won't be anywhere as near as good as who you're used to playing.'

'I'll remember.' He grinned.

'And you have to promise not to laugh at my shots.'

'I wouldn't dare. Just try to relax. I haven't asked you to play golf so I can judge your game.' His eyes roamed over her face. 'Do you have sunscreen on?'

'Oh, no. I totally forgot.' She'd been too busy checking her appearance before she left, trying to make sure she didn't look as if she'd spent ages getting ready which was exactly what she had done. He handed her the sun cream and she rubbed some on her arms and face then up to where her ponytail exposed the skin around the back of her neck.

103

She handing the tube back to Tom who was looking at her with an expression she couldn't read. He reached forward, gently wiping away a dot from her cheek. 'You missed a bit.'

'Thanks,' she muttered, trying to ignore the jolt she felt at his touch.

'Did you bring a jacket or kagoul?'

'Um, yes. The weather looks okay though, doesn't it?'

Tom narrowed his eyes looking out towards the water and Molly followed his gaze. Far into the distance she could see a few scattered clouds but they didn't look threatening.

'Some of that cloud might roll in later but we should be finished by then,' he said, turning to face her. 'Okay, I think we're good to go. You all set?'

'As I'll ever be.' She swallowed.

As they made their way to the first tee, Molly could feel the gentlest of breezes brush against her skin and she took a few seconds to appreciate her surroundings. She couldn't imagine a more beautiful setting for a game of golf. The views of the sea were breath-taking and the fairway stretched out before them, dotted with heather and swathes of yellow gorse.

She inhaled deeply and tried to relax. It wasn't every day she got the opportunity to play with a professional and so she may as well make the most of it. She just hoped he wouldn't think she played too badly, although she knew from seeing him with Luke and Lily that he wouldn't be judgemental, he did seem genuinely concerned that people enjoy the game rather than taking it too seriously.

Tom suggested Molly go first and as she prepared to take her first shot, she felt self-conscious. At least there was no one playing behind them, waiting and watching. She took a steadying breath, remembering all the things her father had taught her and did her best to forget Tom was a professional.

She also tried to forget he was standing so close to her and that he was a man who had the ability to send her heart racing.

Somehow, she managed to focus enough to take her shot, which she had to admit wasn't a total disaster. Feeling inordinately relieved and pleased with herself she slid her gaze over to Tom. He nodded encouragingly and his smile sent a small rush of pleasure through her.

Molly soon realised any attempt to forget Tom was a professional simply wasn't going to happen the moment he stepped up to take his shot. She stood transfixed, watching as he positioned his body, all his focus now on his shot.

Interlocking his fingers around the club and rotating his body on the backswing, he then followed through in one swift movement to strike the ball. Molly saw the muscles flexing in his arms and could hardly tear her eyes from the sheer power of his body. He moved with such confidence and graceful ease, she almost gasped at just how good he was. She knew enough about golf to know that power came from the body, not the arms – she'd been told that often enough by her father – but seeing Tom up close gave it new meaning. He may have been recovering from a broken leg but there was absolutely no doubt this was a man who was a strong and powerful athlete.

His shot flew down the fairway, landing near the flag on the first green and although he'd made it look easy, Molly suspected he wasn't trying particularly hard. They slotted their clubs back into their trollies and started to make their way down the fairway.

Molly was touched that Tom seemed at pains to make sure she was relaxed and enjoying herself and as they walked and talked she finally felt herself begin to relax. Seeing him in what was clearly his natural environment, he was assured and confident but not arrogantly so. He appeared the most relaxed she'd seen him, as if any tension had evaporated.

After watching him take only a couple of shots to get to the next hole, while she took six, she shook her head in exasperation. 'You make it look easy.'

He gave a rueful smile. 'Some days it is. Golf is funny like that

– one day you feel invincible, unbeatable. The next day it's like you've forgotten everything you've ever learned.'

Molly listened with interest. She supposed a bad day at work meant something quite different for a professional golfer.

'But you just have to keep going, despite the difficult days. And then it can all come good when you see that ball soar further than you thought possible, there's something about that moment that golfers live for.' He looked into the distance before turning to Molly with a small shrug. 'Maybe it's not something everyone can understand.'

Molly nodded her head slowly, thinking she could.

When they approached the fifth hole, Tom warned her it was the most challenging of the course. The fairway was extremely wide but then became narrow with a massive bunker guarding the green. As Molly positioned herself Tom came behind her and, with the gentlest of touches, repositioned her shoulders.

'Try to open up your shoulders a little bit and that gives you more height to carry the bunker.'

Slightly distracted by his touch, Molly forced herself to listen to what he was saying and focus on her shot. Following his instructions, she struck the ball and, to her amazement, watched as it landed a few feet from the flag. Her eyes lit up with surprise.

'Wow! Did you see that?' she exclaimed, unable to contain her delight. She turned to find him watching her, his eyes soft.

'That was fantastic.' He smiled then, looking as pleased as she felt.

Molly gave her head a small shake. 'I'll never be able to do that again.'

'You will. Just keep practising.'

Molly wondered if she would start playing again on a regular basis. There were plenty of courses and ranges in and around Glasgow but none with settings which came close to this. When they were halfway round, they stopped for a drink. Tom reached into his trolley to retrieve bottles of water and handed one to Molly.

'Are you enjoying yourself?' he asked her.

'I really am,' she replied honestly. Perhaps even a little too much, she thought.

'There's nothing quite like it, is there? Being out on the course?' she heard Tom's voice. 'I think what I love the most is that everything else leaves my head for a few hours.'

Molly understood that. 'It's so peaceful. No noise, no traffic...'

'...No phone calls or emails,' he added with a smile.

As they finished their drinks and started to walk again, Tom explained a bit more about the course. Like all links courses it followed the natural contours of the land, providing the link between the land and the sea and weaved its way through a natural bird and wildlife haven.

'There's all sorts of wildlife here – the dunes and roughs are full of wildflowers, insects and butterflies. And when the tide is out, you can see seals basking in the sun on the sand banks. I've also seen stoats and weasels – they make their nests in the small gaps.'

'Don't all the spectators trampling ruin it though?' asked Molly.

He shook his head. 'All the courses along the coast act a really important buffer between land and sea and so they take a lot of care to manage and care for the environment.' He smiled lopsidedly. 'Sorry, I can get a bit geeky about all of this.'

Molly shook her head. 'It's really interesting. I'm impressed with your knowledge.'

'I'll be honest, I didn't think too much about all of that stuff until recently. I mean, I've always loved being on the course. But in the last few weeks I've been reading up on it all. There's not much else to do in the hotel room at night.'

Molly's city existence didn't give much rise for thoughts about fauna and flora and such matters but standing there now, with Tom she felt caught up in his enthusiasm. The image of Tom alone in his hotel room at night had also made her thinking go a bit awry.

They played the next few holes in companionable silence and by now were at the furthest away point from the club house. Tom stopped suddenly.

'Look.' He pointed out to the sea. A slight haze hung heavily on the sunlit horizon. 'The haar is coming.'

Molly came to stand beside him. The sky had suddenly darkened and she felt a chill run through her. She had heard of the haar – the old word for a cold sea fog – but had never experienced it for herself. The breeze had strengthened and within minutes the mist had started to swirl in from the sea, creating a blanket over everything and blotting out the sun. Molly couldn't believe how quickly it had all happened. Goose bumps rose on her skin and she started to shiver, feeling cold but strangely exhilarated for some reason.

'Here, take this,' Tom told her, producing a jumper from his trolley. Molly pulled the soft, blue, woollen jumper over her head, catching the faint citrus, masculine scent of him as she did. She hugged it closer to her. It felt safe and warm and she thought she might never want to take it off.

Molly could feel a very fine wet spray touching her face but couldn't actually see it. It was an odd sensation. Where she stood seemed clear – the mist always appeared to be over in the distance. But if she stepped over there, it was gone. It was surreal, like chasing a phantom.

'They say you shouldn't put your head down, but to face up to the haar and you can feel it kiss your cheek.' Tom's words filtered through the mist like a caress and Molly's felt a shiver down her spine. She turned to face him, their gazes locked and the desire to move towards him was overwhelming.

She swallowed deeply and tried to focus on her footing. The visibility was so poor now she could hardly see and the ground beneath their feet felt bumpy and cragged. Molly tried to watch where she stepped but despite her best efforts she still managed to lose her footing, letting out a small yelp as she slipped.

Tom's arms were there, catching her to stop her from falling. Instinctively she clung to him, feeling the tautness of his biceps beneath her fingers.

'You all right?'

'Um, yes. Thanks,' she squeaked. She untangled herself from his arms but was quite happy when he didn't let go of her hand. Her heart was racing and she felt protected by him, safe beside him. He was so close, she could feel the warmth of his body and Molly had the strangest sensation that suddenly they were the only two people in the world, like everyone else had simply vanished.

He tightened his grip of her hand with a reassuring squeeze. 'Don't worry, it will go as quickly as it came.' At that particular moment, Molly wasn't sure if she wanted it to go. She thought she might just want to stay here forever in this world of strange sea mists with Tom.

# Chapter Twelve

Strawberries and Prosecco on a Sunday afternoon in an art gallery was a new experience for Molly and one she could quite easily get used to. She'd never attended the opening of an art exhibition before and it was turning out to be a bit of a revelation. For some reason she'd imagined hushed tones and subdued lighting but nothing could have been further from what she now saw looking around the Red Easel Gallery.

The gallery was a large open space, very light and airy with wooden floors and pale grey walls covered with Freya's paintings. In the background jazz music played, not loud enough to be intrusive but enough to create a relaxed ambience. A black spiral staircase led to a mezzanine level where various art materials had been set out for children to use. There was also another, separate space displaying a range of ceramics, glass and jewellery from local artists.

'You look really pretty, Aunt Molly,' Lily said through a mouthful of strawberry.

'Thank you, Lily, so do you.' Molly smiled, looking down at her.

'Yeah, I forgot you scrub up well, sis,' added Stuart with a grin, putting his arm around her shoulder.

'Ha ha, thanks very much. You don't look so bad either,' she admitted. In fact Molly thought they were all looking smart today. Although Freya had insisted the opening was a casual affair, Anna and Molly had used the outing as an excuse for some girly time and Lily had insisted on giving them facials and nail painting. Molly had sat back while Lily, with surprising capability, had blow-dried her hair so that it fell in soft waves well past her shoulders. Molly recalled all the times Colin had told her she should have it cut shorter. Looking in the mirror after Lily's efforts, Molly ran her fingers over her tamed, shiny locks, glad she had kept it long.

She was also now sporting cherry-red nails thanks to Lily. Not a colour she would normally have chosen but she had to admit, it was working very well with the floral print midi-dress she was wearing.

Molly took a sip of her drink, glancing over at Anna and Stuart. Anna was looking pretty in a floaty chiffon top and more like her old self after the migraine attack. As far as Molly knew, she hadn't made a decision about the job contract but it felt as if a cloud was hanging over her and Stuart in some way.

But for today, Molly was pleased to see them both looking relaxed. They'd received the news that their offer on the town-house had been accepted which had prompted a little celebration at the guest house. Eva, Ben and Jamie had been invited over on Friday evening and they'd all shared a few drinks while the children played in the garden. Eva had also taken the opportunity to share her news. As Molly had suspected, she was expecting a baby. It had been a lovely, happy evening and Molly was thrilled for everyone.

Of course, it was also a sobering reminder to Molly that she needed to think about her future too. She couldn't stay with Stuart and Anna for ever, no matter how lovely it was. She'd been living in a bubble here. A lovely warm bubble. But it wasn't real life. Real life was back in Glasgow where she had to find a flat to rent and a job. But that was for another day, she decided. For now she was happy to enjoy the gallery.

She wandered around, stopping to study the different paintings. They were a mixture of oils and watercolours, each with their own title such as *Rippling Seas* or *Wild Light*. Some were dramatic and stormy, depicting darks skies and threatening clouds, while others were peaceful and idyllic of calm seas and white sands. Molly found herself immersed in the paintings, amazed how the use of light and colour captured the movement of the sea. She decided there and then she was going to buy one. She might not have a house to call her own but when she did she would hang the painting as a focal point and remember her time in St Andrews this summer.

Molly had seen Freya mingling and now she came over to join her.

'Thanks so much for coming,' she said with a wide smile.

'It's a lovely afternoon,' Molly replied. 'And all your paintings are beautiful. I can't believe how they're all seascapes but manage to capture something so different.'

'As an artist I'm lucky to live where I do. The local coastlines provide me with endless inspiration and, of course, the Scottish weather changes by the minute,' she commented wryly.

'That's true,' Molly agreed. 'And I love them all. In fact, I'm going to buy one.' She pointed to a beautifully serene painting with soft blues and greens, tilting her head to study it again. 'Yes, definitely this one.'

Freya looked delighted. 'That's great, I'm so glad you like them. We'll get a reserved sticker on it for you.'

Molly waved a hand to indicate their surroundings. 'To be honest I've never been to anything like this before and I didn't know what to expect. I love the way it's all been set out and it's a great idea to have activities for children.'

'I just think it's really important to make it relaxed and informal – nothing stuffy or pretentious. The owners of the gallery feel the same way so we worked closely on how to set it up. They hold around six exhibitions a year which can be large mixed exhibitions or just solo shows like this one.'

'Well, it certainly works. Please don't let me keep you though – I'm sure you need to circulate.'

Freya nodded gratefully, her eyes scanning the room. 'In fact, I've just spotted the journalist and photographer from the local paper. I better go.'

Molly watched Freya scurry off to speak to the people from the newspaper. One was carrying a camera with a large bag slung over his shoulder and the other held a notepad and pen. They had started to take a few photos and chat to various people including, Molly noticed, Greg Ritchie. She remembered the hotel owner from the other day with Judy. He was well and truly working the room. Constantly moving between people, a touch on the elbow here, a charming smile there.

A glimpse of dark hair made her stop suddenly. She could see Tom. Her jaw almost dropped open when she saw how breathtakingly handsome he looked. She hadn't thought it possible for him to look more attractive but in a white shirt open at the collar and dark trousers he had managed it.

She hadn't expected him to be but now that he was here she felt inexplicably pleased. Molly had felt herself walking on air since her game of golf with Tom. She tried telling herself it had been the joy of playing a game of golf after all this time, but in her heart she knew it was because of Tom.

Unless she had totally misread things – and she had to face it, that was quite possible – she felt sure something had happened on the golf course, something had passed between them. But it was difficult to imagine what came next.

It would be madness to think of another relationship so soon. And yet the more she saw of Tom, the more she thought of what she had had with Colin. Sometimes the way Tom looked at her made her question whether Colin had ever looked at her like that. When she realised he hadn't, it only added to her confusion.

Now that she had seen him, it was impossible not to keep sneaking glances in his direction. Holding a glass in one hand, he was listening politely to the person standing next to him, but Molly sensed he was uneasy. He slid a finger round the back of his collar, the gesture revealing his obvious discomfort.

There was no reason for her not to go over and speak to him. In fact, she felt drawn to him as if an invisible thread lay between them and she wondered if he felt it. She started to make her way over to him when Luke came charging over almost knocking her over. 'Aunt Molly, come and see my drawing,' he pleaded, grabbing her hand.

Recovering her footing, Molly smiled at her nephew. 'Okay, okay. Lead the way.' She looked up briefly to see Tom's eyes on her. His mouth lifted into the smallest of smiles and for a brief second there was no one else in the room. Molly felt a moment of intimacy pass between them and heat flooded her body.

Giving herself small shake, Molly followed Luke and then spent several minutes admiring his picture of a gigantic dinosaur chasing people. She took time to look at the other children's artwork – flowers, animals and houses all conscientiously and lovingly drawn or painted onto coloured paper.

When Molly eventually returned to the main hall Anna and Stuart were in conversation with Tom and she felt her step falter for a second. Stuart was looking relaxed and Tom was smiling at something Anna had said, appearing slightly more at ease than he had earlier. It was odd seeing them together. Two people who were her family, that she knew so well, and the other she had only just met but who was occupying so much of her headspace. She realised as she approached them that she wanted them to like each other, to get on.

'Ah, there you are, Molly.' Anna ushered her in to their little group. 'I've been telling Tom how much Luke and Lily enjoyed the golf range and how they haven't stopped talking about it.'

Molly met Tom's eyes and she smiled at him, memories of their game of golf flickering through her mind.

Stuart waggled his eyebrows at Molly looking pleased with himself. 'And I've got to warn you, Molly, I've decided to book a couple of lessons for myself.'

'Have you?' Molly looked at him in surprise.

'You didn't think I was going to play you without brushing up first, did you? We'll need to have that game soon but don't think I'm doing that without some prior help.'

Molly saw Anna give Stuart a meaningful look. 'We'd better go now and find the children. We're heading back soon.'

Molly narrowed her eyes hoping there was no matchmaking in process here but Anna looked at her innocently.

'We'll see you back at the house, Molly. Nice to see you again, Tom.' And with that, they were gone, leaving Molly alone with Tom.

He looked tired, she thought. Impossibly handsome but tired. She could see shadows under his eyes as if he hadn't slept well and she wondered what might keep him awake at night. There was a hint of stubble covering his strong jaw and she found herself wanting to run her hand along it.

'I—' Molly started to speak but was stopped abruptly by the man she recognised as the journalist barging his way in front of Tom.

'Excuse me. You're Tom Kennedy, aren't you?'

Instantly, a shadow fell across Tom's face, his fist clenched by his side.

'Could we have a moment of your time?' the journalist continued. 'Maybe a few words, possibly a photo?'

Tom's eyes had turned steely cold and his jaw hardened. 'I'd rather not, if you don't mind,' he said tightly.

'Ah come on. Aren't you running the golf school now? Make a great little piece for the paper – hero comes to St Andrews.'

The man with the camera stood poised while the journalist

didn't seem to have any regard for personal space, judging by how close he was standing next to Tom now.

A glint of anger flashed in Tom's eyes. 'Sorry, no,' he said through clenched teeth. He turned to face Molly, touching her arm. 'Listen, would you mind if we got out of here? I could do with some air. Unless you have something else to do?'

'No, nothing planned.'

A few moments later they left the gallery, allowing the stillness and peace to embrace them after the activity and noise of the gallery. Automatically they headed towards the beach. The sun was low in the sky now and the sea shimmered as they strolled along in companionable silence. In one way, Molly supposed it might seem strange that she felt so easy in the company of a man she hadn't known for long but she felt no need to fill the silence and instinct told her that Tom needed some space right now.

Her mind replayed the little altercation in the gallery. There had been no disguising Tom's reaction to the journalist, his unease had been palpable. But even before then he had seemed uncomfortable in the gallery. They continued to walk, the only noise the gentle lapping of the water on the shore until eventually Molly spoke.

'The journalist recognised you. Is that something you get a lot?' she probed gently.

He took a breath and let it out slowly. 'Now and again. The fire – what happened – it's not something I ever talk about.'

'You don't have to—'

He lifted his hand. 'No, it's okay. I—I do want to tell you what happened.'

Molly heard him exhale deeply. He cleared his throat and began to speak, hesitantly at first. 'The tour was in Rome and it was the last night before the final game. It had been a long hot day and I was woken by the smell of smoke and voices shouting. I opened the door but the corridor was full of thick smoke so I ran out to the balcony. I was on the fifth floor and I could see

116

people standing on their balconies above me. I could see they were trapped, there was smoke billowing around them. The only way for them to escape was to try and jump onto my balcony. It was pretty risky but I managed to catch them as they jumped down.'

'That must have been frightening.'

He nodded slowly before continuing. 'But once everyone was on my balcony we realised one of the caddies was missing and must still be on the sixth floor. Someone mentioned something about him taking sleeping pills. I went up to look for him. I put a wet towel over my face and crawled along the floor – the others had told me what room he was in. The smoke was thick and I couldn't see anything. I'm still not sure how I found it.' He paused briefly and Molly could see how difficult it was for him to recall the night. 'I dragged him out to the balcony in his room and by that time I could see a fireman's ladder starting to rescue people from the balcony. The fire was getting closer. I could feel the heat of the flames a few feet away – it was an intense, white-hot heat. All the time I could hear windows smashing all around us. Somehow, I managed to lower him down and then I jumped back onto the balcony. Time was running out and I had to make a leap towards the ladder but the way I landed, I slammed into it at an awkward angle – that's when I broke my leg.'

He frowned, shaking his head. 'I found out later, it was too late for Jim – he had died from smoke inhalation.'

Molly gasped, horrified. She reached over and placed her hand on his arm for a moment. 'I'm so sorry, I can't imagine how awful that must have been.'

'After that it was a bit of a blur.' He shrugged. 'Voices, oxygen, ambulance – the next thing I knew I was waking in recovery.'

Molly could see how difficult it was for him to talk about it, even recalling the fire had taken a lot out of him and a few moments passed before he spoke again.

'Afterwards there was a lot of press about the fire…I managed to avoid it in hospital but later on I was approached for interviews. People started using the word hero.' He shook his head almost in disgust. 'But someone had died. It wasn't about me. I've never talked about it. Until now.'

Molly swallowed, not knowing quite how to respond to that. He had lived through a terrible, traumatic event and that he felt comfortable enough with her to tell her about it felt significant in some way. Or perhaps he had simply needed to talk after a bad day. Either way she hoped it had helped him in some way.

'You risked your life. That was a very brave thing to do,' she said quietly.

He seemed to dismiss the notion. 'Anyone would have done the same.'

Molly doubted that very much, in fact she knew they wouldn't. But clearly, he wasn't comfortable being called a hero as illustrated by the incident with the journalist. And although it didn't take away from what he did, she could understand his reticence and respected it. Physically, he was strong and powerful, yet Molly sensed a vulnerability about him now. Knowing what he had been through made her want to reach out and touch him. But as she glanced at him, she could see he looked spent and realised he had probably said all he could for now.

'Thank you for telling me.'

He glanced sideways at her and breathed in a slightly shaky breath before letting it go. Now the words were out, she could sense that some of his tension had lifted and the strain had left his face.

The sun had dipped lower on the horizon now and Molly could feel the cool North Sea breeze wrapping itself around her bare legs. She shivered, pulling her cardigan closer to her.

'You're cold.' Tom's brow creased with concern.

'A bit,' Molly admitted. 'I don't suppose I'm dressed for an impromptu walk along the beach.'

118

'Probably not.' He glanced sideways at her and she saw his eyes skim over her. 'But you do look very pretty in it.'

'Thanks,' she replied, feeling a blush rise to her cheeks.

The afternoon had turned into early evening now and most people had left the beach. One of the good things about St Andrews was that most things were in walking distance so it didn't take long before they had reached the main hub of the town.

'Are you hungry?' Tom asked suddenly.

'Um, a little bit actually.' Apart from the strawberries, Molly hadn't eaten since this morning.

'Do you like Cullen skink?' he asked.

Molly chewed her lip, thinking. She'd heard of the soup from the town of Cullen but couldn't recall ever trying it. 'Actually, I've never tasted it,' she admitted.

'You've never tasted it?' Tom said, his eyes wide with mock horror.

They had come to a stop outside a small, impossibly pretty restaurant with fairy lights winding their way round the handrail that lead down a few steps to the entrance.

'This place does the most amazing Cullen skink,' Tom enthused. 'It'll be my treat. I feel terrible, dragging you to the beach and making you freeze. Plus you have to put right the wrong that you've never tasted it.'

'Okay, I'll try it if it obviously means so much to you.' Molly gave a little laugh, feeling Tom's hand on her back as he guided her in. Inside was snug and dark with little alcoves and gold thread lanterns hanging low from the ceiling. Molly sat down opposite Tom, a candle glowing between them and their knees almost touching. She tried not to be affected by the intimate setting and the gorgeous man sitting opposite her but wasn't managing too well if her hammering heart was anything to go by.

Molly tried to recall if she'd been alone with a man since Colin left – she must have been, surely. But if so, she couldn't remember. And it certainly wasn't in a setting like this. If you wanted a romantic tête-à-tête she couldn't think of a more private setting. She was very close to Tom. So close she could see the flicker of candlelight dancing in his eyes.

A momentary sensation of guilt passed over her, before she reminded herself she was no longer married. She was a free, single woman and the thought was both liberating and scary. But mostly scary. Because although she was feeling more positive about things, she had no real idea what her future might hold. She gave herself a little shake, taking a deep breath and simply tried to savour the moment.

The soup – made from smoked haddock, potato and onion – was served in deep wooden bowls with hot crusty bread. Molly was famished by the time it came and couldn't wait to taste it. Tom watched as she took her first mouthful of the deliciously creamy soup and widened her eyes in appreciation. 'The flavour's amazing.'

'Told you.' Tom grinned, clearly pleased by her reaction. After finishing her soup Molly sat back in her seat – or at least as much as she could in the small space while Tom ordered them a single malt whisky, apparently the best accompaniment to the soup. Thankfully her heart rate was beginning to settle and Tom definitely looked more relaxed.

'I hope I didn't take you away from the gallery too soon?'

'Not at all, I was ready to leave anyway,' she assured him. 'I really enjoyed it though – I even bought a painting.'

'Yeah? They looked, um, nice.'

She grinned. 'Nice?'

'I don't really know much about art I guess.' He shrugged with a lopsided smile. 'Anyway thanks – for everything.'

At that moment the waitress came to ask if they'd like anything else. After checking with Molly, Tom asked for the bill and then reached for his wallet, leaving a handful of notes on the small silver tray. The sky was velvety black, and the air warm and still as they emerged from the restaurant and Molly realised they had been talking for a long time.

'Is this restaurant a regular of yours then?'

'I eat here occasionally. But only because it's so close to the hotel I'm living in.' He pointed to a small hotel across the road. 'Although I've never been in the company of a beautiful woman before.'

Molly swallowed, managing to stutter a response. 'I loved it, thanks.'

'I'll walk you home,' Tom said.

Molly appreciated the gentlemanly gesture except she knew of course West Sands wasn't her home. It was a beautiful guest house where there would soon be new guests. She felt a stab of something unpleasant at the thought of returning to the city, her sanguinity tinged when she remembered that none of this was real. She tried not to think of the future too much, telling herself to just enjoy this moment of walking with Tom under the stars.

Aware she had fallen silent, she turned to find him studying her.

'You looked miles away there.'

'I was just thinking how much I've love being here.'

'But you're not leaving for a while, are you?'

She shook her head. 'It's strange, I always thought of myself as a city person but being here these last few days, being close to the sea, I think it could get used to it.'

'Do you think you would ever leave the city?' he wondered.

She pressed her lips together, thinking. 'I honestly don't know. I love it here but this isn't reality, at least not for me. In theory I could go anywhere but realistically, I'll probably stick to what I know.' Although for some strange reason, Glasgow didn't feel like home at this very moment.

'At least with my brother living here, I'll be able to visit much more easily than Manchester so it'll be great being able to see Luke and Lily whenever I want. I love being an aunt and…'

'And?' he prompted gently.

'And I was just thinking about how much I would love to be a mother one day. But being divorced before I'm thirty, I'm hardly on track, am I?' She laughed humourlessly, shaking her head. 'God, where did that come from? Ignore me.'

'Did you want a family with your ex-husband?'

'We never discussed it properly which probably sounds a bit odd I know. For me it was something so natural I just assumed he'd want it too.' She gave a small rueful laugh. 'Somehow I don't think messy children would have fitted into his ideal life. Just like I no longer did.'

She felt Tom study her and then he spoke very quietly. 'Do you still love him?'

Molly took a moment to think and could see now their marriage probably wouldn't have lasted. They had grown too far apart and she had fallen out of love with Colin.

'No. I did on our wedding day. But I no longer loved him on our divorce day.'

She glanced sideways at him. 'What about you – do you want a family?'

'If you'd asked me a year ago, all I would have been focused on was the game and winning. But recently…seeing Joe and Beth. I can see how special it is and it *is* something I would want.'

He was looking at her with an expression she couldn't read. They were almost at the guest house now and they paused. Molly looked at him feeling suddenly shy. 'Thanks again – for dinner.'

His eyes briefly roamed her face before he leaned down, and kissed her softy, their lips meeting for an exquisitely brief moment. 'Goodnight, Molly.'

And with her heart thundering in her chest, Molly quietly slipped into the house.

# Chapter Thirteen

Molly was sitting on a chair in the garden, tapping a pen against her notepad as she attempted to wade through the thoughts swirling around her head. She'd been sitting for over half an hour now and had been full of good intentions to write down some ideas, make a few plans but so far she hadn't managed to write a single thing down.

This morning she had updated her CV which she was pleased to see looked healthier than it had a year ago. She'd been mulling over the idea of freelance event work, wondering if that was something she could do. She knew it was a competitive market but she'd made a few contacts now and was pretty sure she'd enjoy the work.

She knew from listening to Anna in the past there were advantages to working freelance – she could choose who she worked for, and work whenever and wherever she wanted. But of course, the downside was not being able to always depend on regular work – not that Anna ever seemed to have that problem.

The junior tournament at Drumloch was tomorrow and then the next day Molly needed to return to Glasgow. Having accepted an offer on the house, the legal work was in motion and she had arranged a meeting with her lawyer. Her parents were flying in a couple of days after that so that would give Molly some time to organise a few things before going to the airport to collect them. She knew the time was approaching for her to make decisions.

The last couple of weeks had passed quickly and busily for Molly, the days slipping into a pleasant pattern. Joe's wife was out of hospital now but still quite poorly so Joe was dividing his time between the school and being at home with her.

Tom and Joe had more or less given Molly free rein to do what she had to and it had been nice for her to come and go as she pleased. Sometimes she came to the range alone, other times she brought Lily and Luke so they could play. Unsurprisingly, Lily was very focused and Molly had derived a certain familial pride at her niece's natural ability with a golf club and had tried to coach her a bit.

Tom was busy taking most of the lessons while Molly focused on the tournament but they had seen each other most days, making time for a coffee and a chat.

It had soon become apparent that apart from taking names, not much else had been done. She had spent some time with Kenny whose computer-savviness had helped enormously and between them they had created a registration form and a spreadsheet to schedule times for the players to go out and play. Molly had made up welcome packs for each player which included scorecards and a list of rules. She had also visited a few local shops and managed to persuade them to donate some prizes in the form of balls, caps and chocolate.

Molly had also popped in to see Judy several times, who was busy experimenting with different drinks for the tournament. As well as her usual variety of soft drinks, she had devised several golf-themed cocktails and Molly and Tom had spent a very pleasurable – and as it turned out, slightly tipsy – afternoon sampling some of her creations. One drink she had named *The Links* was made from whisky, honey, lemon and pink grapefruit, but Molly's favourite had been *The Tee-off* consisting of Glenmorangie, Earl Grey tea, lemon and syrup.

On more than one occasion Molly had found Harry there enjoying a drink and, by the looks of it, Judy's company. So it had come as no real surprise when Judy mentioned Harry would be helping her out on the day of the tournament, which Molly was thrilled about.

Molly had loved it all. Realising just how much she had picked up in the last year at the events company, she relished the opportunity to put some of her newly learnt skills to use.

Slowly she was beginning to feel her confidence grow and she found herself wondering how much of that was because of Tom. The way he listened and talked to her, the way he looked at her, it all made her feel different in some way, perhaps more like the person she used to be.

She sighed now, looking down. Her mind, like the page, was totally blank of ideas. And she knew the reason she was struggling to assemble her thoughts was because of Tom. He was there, colouring all her thinking with possibilities.

With his kiss replaying in her mind Molly was finding it difficult to think about anything else. She cautioned herself from reading too much into it. It had been a spur of the moment kiss, simply his way of saying goodnight.

So why then did she keep thinking of it in quite another way? A kiss capable of making her body tingle just thinking about it, a kiss she sensed could have easily turned into so much more.

She knew she shouldn't let Tom alter her thinking; she had only known him a few weeks and it seemed slightly ridiculous to think he may be a factor in her future. But it was impossible to deny or ignore the intensity of her feelings for him.

She told herself to keep a clear head. She certainly couldn't go rushing into anything else after just coming out of a failed marriage. Instinct told her Tom was a good man, and she would like nothing more than to have her trust restored in men, but the truth was she'd have trouble trusting anyone again. After Colin, she knew she needed to be sure. More than sure. She knew nothing in life came with a guarantee, that the foundations had to be stronger than what she had built her marriage with Colin on. She acknowledged now that she and Colin had married too quickly and if they had waited, time would have told them it was wrong. So she would never rush again – she couldn't get it wrong a second time.

She felt as if something was growing between her and Tom and she found it shocking how much she was drawn to him. Was her body playing tricks on her – was she confusing her physical reaction for something more? But it was more than just the physical aspect. How could she be feeling like this so soon after meeting him and so soon after the end of her marriage? Was something happening between them and if so, wasn't it happening too quickly? Yet even as the doubts mounted up in her mind, she knew just one look, one touch and they would all come tumbling down.

She looked up, hearing a noise, and saw Anna coming towards her clutching two glasses and a bottle of wine. Molly sat up as she approached, noticing she appeared different in some way, a lightness in her step.

'Hello,' Molly said. 'You look happy.'

'That's because I've made a decision.' She plonked herself down on a seat beside Molly.

'Oh?' Molly watched Anna rather ceremoniously pouring wine into the glasses before handing one to her.

'I'm not taking the Forres job,' she announced decisively.

'Oh Anna, I think that's the right decision.' Molly felt relief flood through her, not realising until that moment how much she had been worrying about Anna. 'I think that's the right thing. At least till everything settles with the new house and the children at school.'

'I can see that now. But it's taken a bit of soul-searching.'

'And what did you find?' Molly asked with a small smile.

'Stuart and I had a really good, long chat – in fact, it was the night you babysat. Do you remember?'

Molly nodded, recalling the evening after Anna's migraine that she had finally persuaded them to go out, just the two of them.

'It was a lovely evening – it's been a long time since we'd talked properly. He told me he was worried about me, he thought the migraine might have been my body's way of telling me to slow down. At first I was going to dismiss that as nonsense. But I started to think about the new job contract and deep down I knew my heart wasn't in it. I was taking the job on automatic pilot. I began to realise that without my parents it didn't feel as important anymore.'

'That's understandable,' Molly commented. 'You're grieving and you need to give yourself time.'

'But that's the thing, all the time in the world won't bring them back. I'm not sure I'll ever feel the same. I was their only child and so much of what drove me to work and be successful was to make them proud.'

'Which they were, incredibly so.' Molly had met Anna's parents several times, their love and joy for their daughter obvious for all to see.

Anna stared into the distance. 'Where I grew up, no one was expected to go to university. The other kids thought I was weird because I actually listened in class and wanted to learn. So I learnt to hide it from them otherwise they would have made my life a misery. Of course, I was never in the popular group.'

She brought her gaze back to Molly. 'There was this one girl who seemed to have an inexplicable power over everyone. The boys all fancied her, the girls all wanted to be like her – me included. I got it into my head if I could have a party and invite them all they'd finally accept me. I begged my parents to allow me to have a fifteenth birthday party and of course they agreed. They put up balloons and made food…I was so excited.' She

127

paused. 'And everyone turned up and basically trashed the place. Someone spilt drink all over the sofa...it was awful. But my parents never got angry and I felt so guilty.' Her voice cracked at the memory.

'Oh, Anna.' Molly leaned forward and squeezed her hand.

'After that, I stopped trying to be like one of them. All I wanted was do well and make my parents proud. Now they're not here... well, it doesn't seem as important anymore. Being here...' She waved her hand vaguely encompassing the garden. 'It's given me a new perspective. And I'm ready to do something a bit different.'

Molly saw a glimmer of excitement in Anna's eyes. 'So what are you going to do?' she asked her.

'Well, I thought I would run the two downstairs bedrooms in the new house as a bed and breakfast – at least during the summer.' She clasped her hands together, waiting for Molly's reaction.

'Wow, I didn't expect that, but I think it's a fantastic idea!'

'You do – honestly?'

'Definitely.' Molly grinned. 'The setting here is perfect and you'll have more time to be with the children.'

'That's what I thought. And I can still take some freelance work in the winter if I want. But I'm really excited about the bed and breakfast. I discussed it with Eva to get an idea of what it would really be like. She's offered to help if she can – she's already given me loads of useful information.'

'That all sounds wonderful.' Molly beamed. 'I'm so happy for you.'

'And you being here has helped so much, Molly.'

'What, seeing the mess of my life has helped you?' she joked.

'Don't be daft. You gave us time and having you around has been so lovely. And you know you can come and stay anytime.'

'And I appreciate that so much.' Molly sipped her wine and looked down at the notepad in her lap. Her heart felt lifted for Anna and she hoped now it was her turn to move forward, to find happiness. Was it possible that Tom had awakened something in her – something she'd never felt before, even in her marriage? It was both exhilarating and uncomfortable to acknowledge she hadn't felt like this before. On one level it all seemed confusing and complicated and on the other level achingly simple. What if this was it? What if she'd found someone who she could love and be loved in return? She knew Colin had never made her heart thunder in her chest the way it did with Tom and she had to know if he felt the same. Anything was possible, you just had to be brave enough to try.

****

A few hours later Molly studied her reflection in the mirror. She blinked a few times, her eyes unaccustomed to the lashings of mascara she had coated on her lashes. She had smoothed a layer of subtle foundation to give her skin an extra glow and finished with a touch of lip gloss.

She slipped on a pale pink summer dress, liking its silky feel against her skin and then edged her feet into espadrille wedged sandals. Finally, she clipped a silver necklace around her neck which nestled prettily against her sun-kissed skin.

She declined Stuart and Anna's offer to join them and the children for a pizza, telling them she was taking a leisurely walk to the golf school to check a few final details for tomorrow.

There was a tangible buzz around the town with hundreds of spectators having arrived for the tournament and Molly walked slowly, weaving her way through the crowds, taking her time. She wanted to arrive cool and composed. Not that she had planned what she was going to say to Tom, but she knew it suddenly felt imperative to see him. She might not get an opportunity at the tournament and then the next day she was going to Glasgow.

She felt a quiver of excitement run through her at the thought of seeing him and was almost skipping by the time she approached the school. Her body slumped with disappointment when Kenny told her Tom had already left. Molly hadn't realised it was so late – she'd obviously walked a lot slower than she thought. She stayed chatting to Kenny who was waiting for the last couple of players to finish on the course before locking up and then said she'd see him tomorrow.

Molly smiled to herself, Tom probably wanted an early night before tomorrow. Feeling brave, she thought she might as well see if she could catch him at his hotel. By the time she reached the main street, the town was still busy, a distinct buzz about the place. No one appeared to be in hurry, they were all meandering along at a snail's pace, stopping to look in windows and enjoy the sunshine. Molly had to dodge her way round people, feeling suddenly impatient. She passed the little restaurant that Tom had taken her to, the intimacy of that night flickering pleasurably in her mind.

She froze.

Tom was standing at the entrance of his hotel with a woman. She was slim with a curtain of blonde hair falling over her face. The woman moved in closer to him and Tom wrapped his arms around her in an embrace so tender and gentle that Molly gasped out loud. She wanted to tear her eyes away but was rooted to the spot, unable to move. They pulled apart now and Tom said something, gesturing with his hand for her to go through the door of the hotel before him.

With the most horrible sinking realisation, Molly knew it was Tom's ex. She must be in town with the tournament and have decided to contact him – catch up on old times maybe. Perhaps they realised they still had feelings for each other. The thought that he might be having an early night for quite a different reason made her feel sick.

They had history together so it was understandable if they had decided to rekindle what they had. But what had really hurt the most was seeing the tenderness he so obviously still had for her. The way he had held her seemed to speak a thousand words. The

Tom that Molly had got to know – handsome, sexy and caring – wasn't hers, as much as she now knew she wanted him to be.

Molly blinked. Suddenly it was Colin she saw – Colin with another woman. It couldn't be happening again. How could she be so stupid? She had wondered over the past few weeks if she was imagining something between her and Tom, if it was real. At least now she knew – it wasn't real, at least not for him. He had been nice to her and she had mistaken it for something more. They had shared moments of closeness and she had sensed the promise of so much more to come between them. She thought they had grown close, she thought she knew him, but clearly she didn't know him at all. After the end of her marriage it hadn't been easy for her but she had started to trust Tom, to open up to him. With a sinking feeling she realised she had got it very wrong.

She had the worst judgement in the world. She knew she had fallen for him completely and only now she knew it wasn't going to happen did she feel the full force of her devastation.

She didn't think it was possible for matters to be made worse, but to her horror Tom glanced over. Had he seen her? She felt horribly exposed. Quickly she turned, every fibre of her being screaming at her to move. Summoning all her dignity she turned and started to walk, her eyes suddenly blinded by tears. Concentrating on putting one foot in front of the other, she was barely aware of her surroundings as she returned to the guest house.

With shaky fingers she found her keys at the bottom of her bag, almost sagging with relief that no one was home yet and ran up to her lovely, safe room. Never had she been so grateful to shut a door behind her.

She kicked off her sandals and whipped off her dress, flinging it into a crumpled heap on the floor. The make-up that had taken so long to apply was now scrubbed off in seconds. Moments later she stood under a scalding shower and let the tears flow.

# Chapter Fourteen

Molly squared her shoulders and plastered on a smile, ready for the day ahead.

She'd arrived early at the golf school this morning, armed with coffee and doughnuts for everyone, which had gone down well, especially with Kenny and a couple of his friends who were helping out. Her heart had skipped a beat when she'd seen Tom. Wearing blue chinos and a white polo shirt, he looked every inch the golf professional. She tried to fight it but her body betrayed her, responding to him immediately. Somehow she had managed to keep her distance from him, making sure she was busy elsewhere and turning the other way when she felt his gaze on her.

Last night she had finally gone to bed feeling hollowed out and empty. She had tossed and turned for hours, the image of Tom with his arms around the woman playing over and over again in her mind until finally she had fallen asleep hugging her pillow.

Now she was determined not to shed any more tears. The fantasy was over and she had to deal with reality. She would face her future alone. And why shouldn't she? She was fed up of being scared and unsure. She felt a little surge of independence. She didn't need a man to prop her up or to make her complete. She could do this alone. She just had to get through the tournament today and then tomorrow she would be back in Glasgow.

Taking a deep breath, she looked up at the sky. She had checked the weather forecast countless times over the past few days and only now that she could see the sun shining in a cloudless blue sky with her own eyes did she finally believe it. That was at least one less thing to worry about. Everything was ready and in place for the tournament. It wasn't going to be the day she thought it might have been but she did manage to feel a little rush of excitement thinking about all the children arriving soon.

She had hung some bunting and pinned a few balloons about the place to add a sense of fun and occasion and she had arranged for Kenny and his friends to go and collect a couple of tables from the inn where she set up bottles of water for the children to help themselves.

Kenny was now stationed at the desk in reception ready to tick off the names as the children registered and then Joe was going to break the ice with a brief chat. The children were going to be heading out to play in groups of two or four, leaving at ten-minute intervals, and parents and spectators could follow their offspring round the course if they wished. And of course, they could also go and have a drink at the inn. Lily had made some lovely signs on blue card with gold lettering, directing people through the path towards the inn.

Because players had to be aged at least eight, Molly had devised a few games and activities for their younger siblings. She had sourced some fun emoji golf balls showing happy, laughing or angry faces and some plastic clubs and balls and set aside an area for them on the grass in front of the school.

Molly felt the lightest touch on the small of her back and knew by the small shockwave that shot through her that it was Tom. She turned towards him, trying not to meet his eye. She could feel him studying her.

'Is everything all right, Molly?'

'Of course,' she replied over-brightly. 'Just keeping my fingers crossed it all goes smoothly.'

'I'm sure it will, thanks to you.'

She waved her hand dismissively.

'You look lovely,' he said.

She had dressed carefully today, selecting a green ruffle dress which she knew suited her auburn hair and accentuated her hazel eyes. On the inside she might be a mess but outwardly at least she'd wanted to look her very best.

'You got my text last night?' He frowned.

Not only had she received it, she had stared at his words – asking if they could meet – for a long time wondering how to reply. He knew she had seen him at the hotel so he probably wanted to tell her that he was getting back together with Jen. She didn't really need to hear it. She'd seen enough with her own eyes.

'Sorry I didn't have time to reply – you know, what with my parents arriving and everything.'

'Can we speak later—'

'Oh, look! The first people are arriving,' Molly interrupted, practically launching herself at the little group who were making their way over. She turned briefly to Tom and said, 'Good luck with everything,' before moving away.

Suddenly it seemed as if everyone had arrived at once. The small car park started to fill up as cars parked and groups of children and adults made their way to the school. Molly heard the babble of voices grow and smiled seeing the children's excited faces.

She hovered discreetly until it appeared most people had arrived. Realising she hadn't seen Lily or Luke, she went to check the list of names in reception and saw there were still a few to come anyway, so it wasn't a problem.

Stepping back into the sunshine, she saw them hurrying from the car park. Even from this short distance Molly could see Lily was trailing behind.

'Sorry, we're late,' Anna puffed looking flustered. She shot Molly a meaningful look before glancing over at her daughter. Lily's face was a picture of misery and Molly felt her heart plummet.

'Hi, Lily, are you all set to go?' she asked.

Her niece looked up imploringly at Molly, her eyes brimming with tears. 'I don't want to play anymore, I don't know anyone.'

Molly put an arm around her shoulders, lowering herself down to speak quietly to her. 'Lily, don't be upset. You don't have to play if you don't want to but I really think you would enjoy it. There's lots of boys and girls here who are just like you.'

'But they all know each other,' she said miserably.

Molly stood up and look helplessly at Anna who shrugged her shoulders. 'It took every trick in the book just to get her here but she's determined she won't play,' she whispered.

Hearing a warm familiar voice, Molly turned and felt hugely reassured to see Harry, especially as he was holding the hands of two adorable girls either side of him.

'Hello, Harry.' She smiled.

'I thought we were going to be late – I was forced to stop and eat ice cream on the way here.'

'You are the last here but you're not late at all,' Molly reassured him.

'Hello again, young lady.' He focused on Lily and with some sort of grandad superpower seemed to gauge the situation.

'These are my granddaughters – Olivia and Grace. Now I could be wrong but I think Olivia here might be the same age as you. Twenty-two, is that right?'

'Don't be silly, Grandad.'

The smallest smile escaped Lily's mouth as she looked up at Harry.

'How old are you then? I've forgotten.'

135

The little girl rolled her eyes and shook her head, giggling. 'I'm eleven.'

Anna put her hands on her daughter's shoulders, very gently propelling her forward. 'Hello, Olivia and Grace. This is Lily and she's eleven as well.'

The two girls regarded each other shyly for a moment and everyone seemed to hold their breath waiting until eventually Olivia spoke in a shy voice. 'Would you like to play with me?' she asked Lily. Clearly she had inherited the kind gene from her grandfather, Molly thought. After a quick backwards glance to her mother for a reassuring nod, Lily walked off with Olivia towards the school. Relief flooded Anna's face as she introduced herself to Harry and thanked him.

'All part of the grandad services,' he joked with a wink before heading off with his other granddaughter.

'Phew, that was close.' Anna watched until Lily's figure disappeared into the little throng of bodies. Taking a breath, she looked around. 'Looks like you have a good crowd.'

'Everyone seems to have turned up which is great. And don't worry about Lily, she'll be fine.'

'I'm sure you're right.' Anna took a breath. 'Right, I'd better go and find my son before he starts terrorising the locals. And well done, you. It's going to be an amazing day. I'll see you back at the house,' she called over her shoulder.

Molly allowed herself a moment to survey the scene, experiencing a little surge of satisfaction that everything was up and running. She could see Tom and Joe welcoming the kids and making sure no one felt left out. It was easy to see Joe very much assumed the role as showman, cracking jokes and putting people at ease while Tom was clearly happy to blend more into the background. But there was no doubt they worked well as team. Molly saw Lily and Olivia go over to Tom, his facing lighting up as he recognised Lily. She watched for a moment as he helped her prepare for her first shot. She let out a sigh, desperately trying not to be so affected by him but it felt impossible. She gave herself a shake and turned away.

****

A few hours later Joe appeared at the front of the school with glasses and a bottle of champagne which he passed to Tom to open. Molly watched from a safe distance as he slowly eased the cork out allowing a gentle sigh to escape before filling the glasses for Joe to hand round.

'You old enough to drink?' he joked with Kenny and his friends before passing them each a glass.

'Yeah, prefer a beer if you have one though,' Kenny shot back with a grin.

There were still a few people milling about, seemingly not in a hurry to get home. Not that Molly could blame them. The earlier heat of the day had ebbed away leaving a balmy evening and after all the activity, everything felt calm and peaceful. Molly saw a hare scampering over the green and in the distance she could see swallows swooping over the fairways.

Molly had just waved off Anna and Stuart with the children. Lily's game of golf with Olivia seemed to have gone well and Molly smiled, thinking of her niece's beaming face when she had finished. Olivia's mum had come to collect her and Anna had taken the opportunity to introduce herself and arrange a date for the girls to meet up again.

Molly had gone along to see Judy a few times during the day but really didn't need to. After dropping his granddaughters at the golf, Harry had taken himself along to the inn to help Judy with the drinks and they appeared to have everything under control. Most of the adults had taken advantage of the drinks on offer and the lounge at the inn had been full to bursting at times.

Joe gave a glass to Molly. 'Thanks for all your help today. Seriously, we couldn't have done it without you.'

Molly shook her head, slightly embarrassed.

'I didn't do that much. Everything is already here that you need, it just takes a bit of organising.'

'I think you're being modest. And before I forget, Beth said you must come for dinner one night.'

'That's kind of you.' Molly was touched by the invitation. She had met Beth, who had made a brief appearance today, and had taken to her instantly.

'I'm not sure what my plans are but tell Beth thank you. It was lovely to meet her today.'

Molly sipped at the bubbles and felt her shoulders begin to relax. She felt a small swell of pride that she'd been part of today and that it had gone so well. She also recognised that there was massive potential to do so much more with the school and all its facilities. Today had been small scale but once they had someone to organise it all properly and it was online there was no end of possibilities. She genuinely hoped it all worked out for Tom and Joe.

She watched as Joe continued to make his way through the group, smiling and jesting. Earlier, there had been a small presentation and he had been in his element giving out prizes as the adults looked on clapping. He had announced the winner of the raffle to a couple who had looked quite elated with their prize of dinner for two and a night at the inn. Molly thought it sounded wonderfully romantic and couldn't help feeling a little wistful.

Molly knew it was almost time for her to go. She had an early start and she still wanted to pop in and see Judy on her way back. Despite herself, she sneaked a glance over at Tom before she left. He was leaning against the wall and Molly knew from the way he was standing he was taking some weight from his leg. He lifted his glass to take a drink and as he lowered it, his eyes caught hers. Quickly she averted her gaze. It was definitely time to go.

****

The light was beginning to fade as Molly walked along the path to the inn and she could see the trees silhouetted against the darkening sky. She suddenly felt very tired and a nightcap with Judy sounded just what she needed.

'Molly.'

She stopped, her heart thumping, and listened to Tom's footsteps close in behind her. He came to stand in front of her and she desperately tried not to meet his eyes, for fear that she would melt. Only hours ago she had wanted to see him desperately, she'd had so much she wanted to say to him. Now she didn't know what there was to say. Her defences had gone up, all her doubts had risen to the surface.

His blue gaze settled on her, his expression earnest. 'You came to my hotel yesterday?'

She tucked a strand of hair behind her ear, adopting a casual tone. 'I happened to be passing that way.'

'Was it to see me?' he asked ignoring her attempt at indifference.

She felt her shoulders slump, feeling suddenly deflated. 'No. Maybe. But it doesn't matter now.'

'Listen, I want to tell you—'

'You don't owe me any explanations. I'm happy for you and your ex—'

'My what?' He stared at her.

'The woman at the hotel.'

'You thought that was Jen?' He sounded slightly incredulous.

'Wasn't it?'

'No.'

'Oh.' Molly looked at the ground for a moment digesting this but knew it didn't really matter. If it wasn't Jen then it was still some other woman.

'That's why I texted wanting to see you, to explain who she was. The woman you saw, she was Jim's wife. He was the caddie who died in the fire.'

Molly's hand flew to her mouth, horrified at her mistake. 'I thought, I assumed…'

He ran a hand over his face and took a breath, releasing it slowly. 'She contacted me to say she'd been asked to present a trophy in his memory at the Scottish golf awards dinner. She assumed I'd be there too.'

'But you didn't want to go?' Molly guessed correctly.

'I was invited but I knew I wouldn't be comfortable – I hate these things. People tend to want to talk about the fire…the rescue. When I told her I wouldn't be there, she asked to see me. I'd met her briefly once or twice over the years but hadn't seen her since the fire.'

Molly swallowed. 'That must have been difficult, meeting her.'

'It was. She talked about Jim and how happy they'd been together…and she thanked me for trying to save him.' He closed his eyes for a moment and it took Molly every ounce of her willpower not to go to him. 'She's trying to get on with her life. They have a daughter so she has to keep going for her. But I wanted to meet her because I . . . I thought it might help me to move forward too.'

There was a pause and Molly spoke quietly. 'And did it – help you?'

'I think so. That's why I wanted to speak to you. I think – at least I hope – we have something between us, Molly. But there's so much I need to try and explain to—'

Molly took a step away, shaking her head. She didn't want to hear anything, didn't want to risk being drawn to him anymore. 'Tom, it doesn't matter now. It's too late.'

Tom raked a hand through his hair, looking helpless. 'Why is it too late?'

'When I came to your hotel, I was coming to tell you that I had feelings for you. I was worried that it had all happened too quickly after the end of my marriage but I thought maybe you felt it too. But when I saw you, I thought…' She paused, taking a breath. 'I'm sorry for jumping to the wrong conclusion, I really am. But I know now I'm not ready to trust again. I'm not ready to move on. It's too soon for me. I'm sorry, Tom.'

'I'm not suggesting we rush into anything. Only to give us a chance.'

'I . . . I can't.' She shook her head. There was a single step between them and Molly knew that was all it would take. But she couldn't do it. How could she when her trust was so fragile – it was too difficult.

'Goodbye, Tom.'

****

As she opened the door of the inn, Judy rushed by carrying a plastic linen basket piled high with what looked like sodden towels. Her usually perfectly coiffured hair was distinctly dishevelled and there was a spot of colour on each of her cheeks.

'Judy?'

'Oh Molly, hello,' she said distractedly. 'I just need to deal with these.' She nodded her head at the basket. 'Can you come with me?'

'Of course.' Molly followed her through to the little warren of rooms behind reception. They entered a small laundry room which housed an industrial washing machine and tumble dryer. Judy spilled the contents of the basket into a massive stainless-steel sink and then turned, leaning against it gratefully. Molly let her draw breath before speaking. 'What on earth happened?'

'I'll show you,' Judy said gloomily. 'It's been such a busy day and after everyone left I was very tired,' she explained as Molly followed her up the wide carpeted staircase to her small living quarters.

'I decided to take a bath so I poured in some bubble bath and came through to the living room just to take the weight off my feet and...' Her voice faltered as she opened the door to the bathroom where the smell of damp and warped floorboards pretty much told Molly what had happened before Judy confirmed it.

'And I fell asleep. When I woke up, I realised straight away I'd left the taps running. I rushed through but of course it was too late.' She waved her hand vaguely to encompass the damage where the water had surged over the top of the bath and soaked the entire floor.

They stood in silence for a moment surveying the damage.

'I've mopped up most of it so I'll just have to wait for it to dry off now. I'll need to redecorate the whole room,' she sighed.

Molly regarded Judy with concern, hoping today hadn't been too much for her. 'What can I do to help?' she asked.

'I can't sleep here tonight – everything's a bit damp and musty smelling. One of the guestrooms is empty, I'll sleep there I think. I was airing the bed though so would you mind helping me make it up? It suddenly feels a bit of an effort to do on my own.'

'Of course.'

Judy fetched fresh linen and then went with Molly to the empty bedroom.

'What a beautiful room!' Molly exclaimed. The floors were carpeted with rich opulent rugs and a solid oak bed sat in the middle of the room. In the corner there was an antique dressing table with decorative brass lamps.

Judy looked up from unfolding the sheets. 'Yes, it is rather special, isn't it?'

Molly copied Judy's movements as she pulled the sheet and expertly tucked it into the corner to produce a tight diagonal fold 'That's a very professional finish,' Molly commented.

'I like it to look a certain way although I'm not sure why I'm bothering when it's for only me,' she said smoothing down the wrinkles now of the goose-feather duvet.

'At least you'll have a good night's sleep here.' Molly realised how fond she'd grown of the older woman and didn't like the idea of leaving Judy.

'I have an appointment tomorrow in the city but I wish I could stay and help.'

'That's so kind of you, dear, but I'll be fine. I have a lady who comes in the morning. Now, how about a little drink before you go?'

Molly smiled her approval but wished the day had ended on a happier note – not just for her but Judy too.

# Chapter Fifteen

The silence of the house screamed at Molly as she stepped through the front door. The air felt cold and unlived in and she felt a chill go through her. She bit down on her lip, totally unprepared for the rush of emotion that engulfed her. She could hardly believe she'd only been gone a few weeks, it felt so much longer.

When she had last been here she still regarded it as home. Not one with the happiest memories but home nonetheless. Now, it reminded her too much of Colin and their failed marriage. She knew she was ready to leave and any attachment she may once have had to it was now gone.

Technically it was still her house – well, hers and Colin's – until the legal papers were all signed. Soon a new family would move in. The estate agent told her a family with two children had bought it and Molly had been delighted. They would fill the rooms with love and happiness the way she and Colin had never managed.

She gathered up the post lying on the mat, adding it to the pile on the hall table which the estate agent must have left. She would sift through it later. For now, she needed a hot drink and went to the kitchen to fill the kettle. Everything felt so still and quiet after being at the guest house. No other voices or footsteps, just silence.

Her body felt strangely jetlagged and out of sorts, as if she'd travelled from a faraway place in a different time zone instead of just a few hours in the car. She felt like she was in no-man's land, caught between two places. One where her heart was and one where her head was. In a way St Andrews *was* another world, certainly very different from life in the city.

She thought now of St Andrews, of the pretty shops and cafés and the cobbled streets. She thought of Judy and the little inn nestling in the trees. She thought of the golf courses and the beautiful stretches of sand by the sea. And she thought of Stuart and Anna starting their new life there with the children.

And she thought of Tom. When she'd arrived in St Andrews she had been frightened and hurt. But then over the next few weeks she had slowly started to live again. She realised she hadn't just been going through the motions or having to put on a brave face. Her fake smile had become a real one. And it had been because of Tom. He had made her start to remember who she was and perhaps for that she should be grateful. Now, she had to forget him and move on.

She leaned against the worktop waiting for the kettle to boil. She was lucky, she told herself. She had her independence, her health and she had options. She was a free agent and didn't even necessarily have to stay in Glasgow. But here there was familiarity and friendly people in a city she knew well. She was fairly confident she could either find another job or try a shot at freelancing for a while. She could reacquaint with old friends, start again. The money from the sale of the house meant she could afford to rent a decent place until she found somewhere permanent. She could make life work here.

She popped a teabag in a mug and poured in boiling water, a small glimmer of optimism emerging on her horizon. She squished the teabag against the side of the mug, not relishing black tea but in the absence of fresh milk it would have to do.

It was going to take a lot of energy to sort through what had to be done and a list of all the practical things she needed to do ran through her mind at dizzying speed. The enormity of her future lying ahead of her now fully hit her. It was all down to her and she was going to have to make it work. She had a meeting this afternoon with the solicitor and she intended to go over every single detail. She wanted to make sure Colin never had a reason in the future to come back and claim she had kept anything from him. And so, rallying her strength, she shrugged off her jacket and armed with her tea and a pen and paper went to make a list of things to do.

****

Two days later Molly was exhausted. She had done as much as she could in the time she'd had. The meetings with her solicitor and the estate agent had gone well and she'd even looked at a couple of rental flats in the West End. One in particular had caught her eye, overlooking the Botanic Gardens and for the first time she could picture herself living there on her own.

She'd emailed Colin, letting him know how much the house had sold for, and he remained as resolutely uninterested as before.

At the end of two days she couldn't say she was happy exactly but by the time she drove to the airport to collect her parents this morning, she at least felt satisfied with what she had achieved.

Her parents' flight had been delayed and so Molly had paced the arrivals lounge, consuming too much coffee and indulging in some people-watching.

When Brian and Carol Adams finally arrived, Molly somehow managed to hold herself together, avoiding her mother's assessing gaze and busying herself with their bags and comments on how well they looked – which they did. Life in the Portuguese sunshine was clearly agreeing with them.

The car journey back to St Andrews was long. The roads were jammed with cars full of keen spectators flocking to see the golf.

Molly kept up a stream of banal conversation, anything to avoid mentioning Colin and the divorce.

When they'd finally stepped through the door, West Sands Guest House had erupted into hugs and shouts from the children who were giddy with excitement at the arrival of their grandparents. That had been followed by a noisy and talkative dinner as they all caught up with each other over a delivery of pizzas.

Earlier, her father had taken her aside. Never one for excessive words, he had held her at arm's length, studying her for a few moments before pronouncing she was going to be fine. He'd asked her a few financial details to make sure everything was in order and seemed impressed by the way she'd handled it.

'You're going to have speak to your mother, you know,' he had said sagely.

'I know,' Molly sighed. 'But I'm exhausted tonight.' Which wasn't a lie and so, making her excuses, she escaped the melee of the house to seek refuge in her room. She was bone tired and, to top it all, thought she might have a cold.

She sank gratefully onto the bed, thinking how much she was going to miss this lovely room. Her eyes were almost closing when the knock came.

'Come in,' she called, knowing exactly who it was.

Molly sat up as her mum came in, balancing two cups and a plate piled with slices of cake. Looking effortlessly stylish in white trousers and a checked shirt, Molly had to remind herself that her mother was over sixty. She also had a look in her eye that told Molly the time had come to talk.

'I thought you might be hungry – you didn't seem to eat much at dinner.' She studied her daughter, concern etched on her face.

'I've got a bit of a cold, that's all,' Molly reassured her.

'Anna made these with Lily earlier.' Carol inclined her head towards the cakes as she took a seat beside Molly. 'They're delicious so you need to eat some before I demolish the lot.' She made a face, patting her flat stomach.

'You don't need to worry, Mum. I was just thinking how good you look.'

'Thank you, darling.'

Tempted by the cherry and almond slices, Molly took one from the plate. 'Where's Dad?' she asked.

'Last I saw him he had just started playing Monopoly with the kids. I think he could be gone for some time,' she chuckled.

'You're right, these are good.' Luckily Molly swallowed a mouthful of cake just in time before succumbing to a fit of sneezing.

'Bless you!' Molly took the tissue her mother handed her, marvelling at her ability to produce a clean tissue in any situation as if by magic.

'Thanks,' Molly sniffed, suddenly very grateful to have her mother here.

'So, are you ready to tell me why you've been avoiding me?'

Molly met her mother's eyes and under the full beam of her scrutiny, fell silent. She couldn't deny it, she'd been avoiding her and now realised how ridiculous it sounded. She looked away, shrugging uselessly.

'I have been worried about you, you know,' she heard her say now. 'Your father had to stop me more than once coming to see you. But he's a wise man who knows his daughter well so I listened to him and took his advice.'

'Which was?'

'To leave you alone as you wanted – to give you time.'

Molly looked down. 'I didn't mean to cut you off. I suppose I just wanted to deal with it by myself.'

'That's what Dad said, that you needed time to work through it.' Her mother paused before continuing. 'But you do know you could have come to me anytime, don't you?'

Molly blanched at hearing the hurt in her mother's voice. In the wake of Colin leaving she'd been so busy wallowing in her own misery and shame, she hadn't thought of how that might make her mother feel.

'Oh, Mum, of course I do. And that means so much to me. It's just…' She picked at the tissue in her hand. 'I was so ashamed.'

Carol tilted her head, frowning. 'Ashamed? Why on earth would you be ashamed?'

Molly took a breath as she recalled the days and weeks she had spent coming to terms with the end of her marriage, trying to find the words to explain.

She'd put it off for so many reasons. Reasons that made sense to her at the time but now, seeing the look of love and concern on her mother's face, she was having difficulty explaining them.

While she knew plenty of people whose parents tried to cajole them into making certain choices, Molly's never had. That they had trusted her in some way had put more pressure on her to make the right decisions for herself. She remembered one particular wine-fuelled evening after Colin had left, even blaming her mother for not warning her that this could happen.

'When I married, I wanted what you and Dad have. I thought it would be easy. You met someone, you fell in love. Then you married and lived happily ever after.' She let out a sigh. 'But after a while, Colin and I started to grow apart – even before his affair. I worried we had married too quickly but I was scared to admit I had made a mess of things.'

'You haven't made a mess of anything.'

'I felt like I let you down in some way. As if I was incapable of finding love like you and Dad. And Stuart and Anna.'

'Oh, Molly, you should never have thought that.' She shook her head sadly. 'Although I do admit, sometimes I did worry that Colin wasn't the right man for you.'

Molly looked up. 'You did? Why didn't you say anything?'

'I do recall telling you not to rush into anything. But I would never tell you how to live your life.' She pressed her lips together for moment. 'I remember when I met your father.'

Molly nodded patiently, having heard the story many times of how her parents met. Molly's mother had been living in London when she'd met Molly's father, an engineer working on a huge rail project in the capital. After his job had finished they had married and returned to her father's beloved city of Glasgow.

'It was like nothing I'd ever felt before. Everything fell into place. He made me feel whole, like I'd been looking for something and didn't know what it was until I found him.' She paused for a moment, fidgeting with her bracelet. 'And you have to remember that good can come from bad.'

Molly narrowed her eyes watching her mother. There was a feeling of something unsaid hanging between them. 'Mum?'

'There's something I need to tell you.' Molly felt a ripple of alarm, hoping nothing was wrong with one of her parents.

'I don't suppose there's an easy way to say this so I'll just come out and say it.' Carol swallowed. 'Before I met your father, I . . . I was married. To someone else.'

Molly blinked as she felt her heart drop to somewhere near her feet. She couldn't have heard correctly. 'What do you mean? Why…I don't understand.'

'I married a man I didn't love,' her mother stated simply with a shrug. 'My parents were good people – old-fashioned, working class, who just wanted the best for me. So when I met Simon they were beside themselves. He was well-spoken and well-educated – a man with prospects they called him. My mother's mantra was always "love doesn't pay the bills" and I remember her telling me I'd be a fool to let him go. I married with my head, not my heart. It didn't last a year.' She looked at Molly. 'And that's why I never said anything to you. I was determined I would never interfere with your choices the way my parents had done.'

Molly stood up and paced the floor, not capable of saying much. Her head was swimming and she felt as if the foundations of her life had shifted in some way. She felt a swell of anger grow inside her and turned to face her mother.

'Is there anything else you haven't told me?' she demanded.

Her mother shook her head. 'No, of course not.'

'Does Stuart know?'

'No. But now that I've told you, I'll find the right moment to tell him as well.'

Molly frowned. 'Why didn't you tell me before?'

'There was never a reason to, it was never relevant. I'm telling you now because I hope it will help you. Like me, you married with the best intentions but that doesn't guarantee it will work. But the truth is that you are more than your divorce. You're a kind and wonderful person whether you are divorced or not.'

Molly nodded mutely. Growing up she had always taken for granted her parents' quiet love and devotion. She looked out of the window, her mind racing through all the years of living with her parents to see if she could find any evidence of what she had just found out. But there was nothing.

After a contemplative silence Molly sat down beside her mother again. They regarded each other and slowly comprehension dawned on Molly that what her mother had told her didn't change anything. She and her father had gone on to have a happy life together and that was all that mattered. She swallowed down the lump in her throat and smiled 'Thanks for telling me, Mum.'

'You deserve love and happiness and I know you will find it.'

Molly looked down at the now shredded tissue in her hand. 'I thought maybe I had.' Her voice was so quiet Molly wasn't sure if she had actually spoken the words out loud.

Her mother looked at her questioningly.

'But well, it was complicated.' God, she hated that expression but honestly couldn't think of another way to describe her feelings for Tom.

Her mother spoke gently. 'If it's meant to be, then the confusion, the doubts will all be brushed away. Just trust in yourself. Don't be scared, Molly.'

Molly looked up, her eyes wide with tears, finally letting herself be lost in her mother's embrace.

# Chapter Sixteen

The next day Molly found Stuart sitting at the kitchen table with a pot of coffee, a mound of buttery toast and a pile of scholarly looking documents in front of him.

'Good morning.'

'Morning. Where is everyone?' Molly asked looking around.

'Mum and Dad have gone to watch the day's play at the Old Course and Anna and the kids left with them to go and do more shopping for tonight.'

'More? Don't we have enough already?'

The kitchen was already groaning with food and drink. Deciding to make the most of the continued good weather and having everyone at West Sands, Anna was planning a barbecue for that evening.

'Apparently not,' he said good-naturedly refilling his coffee cup. 'So what are you up to today?'

'I'm going to take a walk and see Judy at the inn.'

'Well, as long as you're back in time to see my barbecue skills in action.'

'How could I possibly miss that?'

After sitting with Stuart for a while, Molly walked to the inn and as she entered, remembered the very first time she came here.

It was all so familiar to her now but just as enchanting. A sumptuous display of purple freesia and white roses sat in a large vase on the desk, their floral scent filling the air.

Judy came bustling out from behind the desk. 'Molly!' she exclaimed.

'How are you, Judy?'

'I'm very well. Have you got time to sit and have a drink?'

'Naturally.' Molly smiled.

Soon they were installed in sofas in the lounge and Molly eyed Judy as she brought over glasses of passion-fruit juice for them. She looked a different woman from the one she had seen the night of the flooded bathroom. Her perfectly poised countenance was fully restored and there was a definite glow about her.

'How's your bathroom now – is there anything you need help with?'

'It's all sorted now, thank you.' Molly noticed Judy's expression soften. 'Harry came round the next day and helped me. He brought a dehumidifier so everything's dried out now. I'll have to think about new flooring but it's certainly not as bad as I originally feared.'

'That's good, I'm pleased.' smiled Molly smiled.

'Harry wasn't the only visitor I had that day,' Judy continued.

'Oh?'

'Greg Ritchie came to see me the day after the tournament. He'd heard all about it being a success and obviously decided it would be a good time to ask again if I'd be interested in selling. We had a little chat and some of what he said got me thinking.'

Molly's heart sank, she knew what was coming. Judy was going to sell the inn.

'He pointed out that there was so much potential for the inn. But it needs someone with energy and vision. Someone younger than me.'

'You're not old, Judy.' Molly frowned.

'That's kind of you to say. But I'm certainly not young. I admit he caught me at a weak moment and I've thought a lot about what he said.'

'So you've decided to sell?' Molly gulped. She didn't know quite why it saddened her so much. She was sure Greg Ritchie would do a good job, he was an experienced hotelier. But this had been Judy's dream with her husband. There was a story behind it and that made it special.

'Like I said, I need someone with energy and vision.'

Molly looked down and nodded silently.

'Which is why I'd like to know if you would be interested in coming to work here?'

Molly's head snapped up. 'Me?'

Judy took a sip of her drink, giving Molly a few moments before slowly setting her glass back down.

'You've probably noticed Harry and I have become quite friendly recently. It turns out he used to run a specialist travel agency and we have a lot in common.'

Molly smiled. 'That's nice for you.'

'We both lost the loves of our lives and know that we'll never replace those people. But we also both know we're at the stage when we need to make the most of our time now. We get on well and would like to spend more time together.'

Molly could easily understand that and thought they would make such a lovely couple.

'So I have a proposition for you. Harry has a brother in New Zealand who he'd like to visit but he hasn't wanted to make the trip on his own. I haven't had a break from this place since George died so I'd like to go with him. Our plan would be to go for a couple of months. I'd only go if I could find the right person to manage the inn. And I'd like that person to be you.'

Molly opened her mouth and closed it. The offer was so unexpected and her mind wheeled trying to take it in. Part of her was very tempted and wanted to jump at the chance there and then. Staying here, working at the inn...so much about it sounded appealing. But there was also a voice of caution in her head and she knew she had to think carefully before making a decision.

As if reading her mind, Judy told her she didn't want an answer straight away. 'I know you have things to consider. But if you decided to stay, you could live in my flat for the time I was away and when I come back we can see how things are. I saw how you dealt with the tournament and I'd be very keen for you to develop some of your ideas. I have every confidence in you.'

Molly gave her head a small shake. 'It's an amazing offer. And I'm honoured that you would trust me. I'll think about it very seriously and let you know, if that's okay?'

'Of course.'

After she left the inn, Molly walked back to the guest house in a slight daze as she mulled over Judy's offer. So much about it was right and she would relish the challenge of working and developing her ideas at the inn. The day of the tournament had proved to Molly what she had suspected. The inn had heaps of potential especially with the golf facility nearby. Greg Ritchie clearly recognised it too and if he could make it work, then why couldn't Molly? She could already feel her imagination alight with ideas.

But then she felt herself land back in the real world with a thump. How could she possibly consider working there with Tom being so close by? She blew out a long sigh, feeling a muddle of confusion and contradiction weighing her down.

By the time she got back to the guest house, preparations were already underway for the barbecue and she went to her room, taking a few minutes to compose herself, determined not to let any of her inner turmoil spill over into this evening. She dressed for comfort, choosing faded jeans and an oversized pink jumper. She twisted her hair into a ponytail, soothed something that promised instant radiance onto her skin and headed downstairs.

\*\*\*\*

West Sands Guest House looked beautiful. The evening sunshine bathed everything in a warm golden glow, making it the perfect setting for a family holiday and worthy of an advert for the Scottish Tourist Board.

The kitchen was a hive of activity. Anna was bustling about looking as if a weight had been lifted from her shoulders. Molly didn't think she had ever seen her look so relaxed.

'Top up?' Anna offered, coming over to where Molly was standing chopping tomatoes.

'Yes please.' Molly inclined her head towards the window. 'It's lovely to see Olivia here with Lily,' she commented. Anna followed her gaze where the girls were together in the garden.

'I didn't want to foist them on each other but they do seem to be getting on well,' Anna said.

Sitting nearby at the table were Molly's parents. Earlier, she had listened to them enthuse about their day at the golf. They'd had an amazing day but were now sitting gratefully in the shade with a drink. Stuart was tending to the barbecue, a fork in one hand and a lager in the other, keeping an eye on Luke who was surrounded by what looked like half the contents of a toy shop.

There was a feeling of everything coming together, Molly thought. As if West Sands Guest House had sprinkled a little magic over everyone. She forced down the uncomfortable feeling of being on the outside looking in. She wasn't going to do self-pity. Instead she felt grateful to be here with everyone. Family – that's what it was all about.

She swiped the tomatoes from the chopping board into the wooden salad bowl with the rest of the ingredients and mixed in some dressing. 'I'll take this out now, shall I?'

'Yes please and can you grab these napkins too? I'll be out in a sec.'

Anna's head turned at the sound of the knock at the door. 'That'll be Ben and Eva. I'll go.'

The air was warm and breezeless as Molly stepped into the

garden. The table was already crammed with all manner of delights and Molly smiled to herself. Anna had enough here to feed the whole town.

Molly let out a little small yelp of surprise as the slightly mad dog from next door hurtled past her followed closely behind by Jamie en route to Luke at the bottom of the garden. Molly turned her attention back to the table, shifting a few things about to make way for the salad bowl.

'There's someone here for you.'

Molly's head shot up hearing Anna's voice. 'For me?' She frowned.

'It's Tom,' Anna whispered, barely containing her glee. 'He's waiting in the front room.'

With her heart racing, Molly walked back towards the house, stopping briefly to greet Eva and Tom in passing. Between her mother's revelation and Judy's job offer, her head was already in a spin. Knowing Tom was here made her legs suddenly feel quite weak. The front room was silent and cool and Molly blinked as her eyes adjusted to the darker light. Tom stood at the window and even from a distance she could see the tension coiled in his shoulders. He looked tired and sombre. And so beautiful, Molly had to steel herself.

Tom looked at her with a guarded smile. 'Hello, Molly.'

'Hello.'

She walked over to the window, preferring to keep some space between them. She stared out at the sweep of white sand and the seagulls circling over the shimmering sea.

'Molly, can we talk?'

'I don't think there's anything more to say, Tom.' She turned to him and she felt her armour weaken on seeing the weariness in his face.

'Would you like a drink? I can get you something.'

His eyes softened. 'Molly, please just sit beside me.'

Molly bit her lip, letting him gently take her by the hand and lead her to the sofa.

157

He took a long breath before slowly releasing it. 'You said it was too soon for anything to happen between us. But before you go back to the city or make any decisions, I need to tell you how I feel.' He hesitated. 'And . . . and I want to tell you what happened after the fire.'

'After the fire?' Molly asked.

'I told you how I recuperated at my mother's house.'

She nodded silently.

'It wasn't the easiest of times but I got through it – physically at least. After a couple of weeks, the fire started to replay over and over in my mind. It was as if I was trying to work out if there was something I could have done differently. Every time I closed my eyes all I could see were the flames and smoke. Then I . . . I started to have nightmares. Terrible nightmares. It's difficult to describe to you how awful they are. How real and frightening.' He paused, looking down.

'Once my leg healed and I moved to St Andrews, I thought somehow the nightmares and flashbacks would all just disappear. I thought if I ignored them, they'd go away. But of course they didn't. If anything, it got worse. I didn't know how to handle it, it was alien for me to think I couldn't cope. It went against everything I'd ever taught himself, the mental strength I'd developed for my game.'

Molly listened carefully. She knew how difficult the fire had been for him, she'd seen for herself how tense he could become but she certainly hadn't appreciated how much he must have been suffering in its aftermath and quite how much of a toll it had taken. She couldn't help feeling disappointed he hadn't felt able to share it with her. 'Why didn't you tell me? I would have understood and wanted to help.'

He ran a hand down his face. 'I could barely admit it to myself let alone tell anyone else. But I've done a lot of thinking recently. I can see now that since the fire, I've been functioning, doing what I have to. But at times it feels like I'm existing – not living.'

He paused to look at Molly and the intensity of his gaze seem to make everything else in the room fade away. 'Then I met you. And everything changed. From that very first moment I met you, I started to fall in love with you.'

Molly felt as if she had stopped breathing.

'But I tried to fight my feelings for you. How could I even consider a relationship while I was battling to get through each day? I didn't want to let you down or be a burden.

'I've done a lot of thinking recently.' His brow furrowed and he gave his head a small shake. 'I was remembering my dad teaching me to ride a bike. It was a present for my eighth birthday – it was second-hand and the blue paint was chipped but I loved it. He took me out this day, holding onto the back of the bike and following behind me. He let go and obviously I lost my balance and fell off. "Get back up, son. Keep going," he told me.

'So I got back on and the same thing happened except this time I grazed my knee. The same thing kept happening and after a while, I wanted to stop, I wanted to cry. But I would never dare cry in front of him. He wasn't a demonstrative man, not the type of man to tolerate his son crying. I've often wondered over the years what he would have made of his son playing golf. If he would have been proud, admired the dedication it took or if he'd dismiss it as a cushy way to make a living.

'Every morning after another nightmare, all I could hear was his voice, telling me to get on with it. Not to be weak.'

Tom's eyes were deep pools of anguish and Molly felt her heart break for him as he turned to look at her.

'I've been running away from the truth for the last year but I'm not running anymore. I wanted you to know everything. Most of all, I wanted you to know how much I've fallen in love with you. I know we haven't known each other long but I've never felt like this before.'

Molly stood up, her mind trying to sieve through everything.

159

She moved over to the fireplace, hearing sounds filtering through from the garden. Happy sounds of family and friends on a summer's evening.

'The difficulties you're having – they wouldn't have made a difference to how I felt. What matters is telling me the truth, never hiding things from each other,' said Molly.

She saw him swallow. 'I should have told you, I should have been more open with you. It's difficult for me to admit that I might need help. I wanted to be with you so much. I wanted to spend the night with you—' His voice broke huskily. 'But I didn't want you to see me like that.'

Molly looked down, absently picking at the sleeve of her jumper. 'After Colin left, I was scared. When I saw you with someone else at the hotel, I froze. I married the wrong man and then I thought I'd fallen for the wrong man. Colin took away so much of who I was, tried to change who I was. I thought I needed to find out what I'm capable of myself – by myself.'

'The right person would never hold you back, prevent you from being what you're capable of.' Tom lifted himself from the sofa and came to stand by her before he continued. 'Do you remember the day on the beach, when you were crying? I remember thinking – apart from wanting to deck your husband – I wanted to say to you that I would never make you cry. I'd always want to make you smile. Your eyes had been full of hurt and pain but eyes as beautiful as yours should be lit up with light and happiness.'

'Oh, Tom.'

'Knowing you might be here for me gives me strength. It makes me feel like anything is possible. And I want to try and make you happy too. I'm so in love with you, Molly.' He took her hand in his and Molly had no desire to pull it away, now or ever. In that moment Molly felt herself step out of the shadow of her marriage and her heart explode with love for Tom.

'You are?'

'Totally. You're beautiful and caring and I want to be with you, Molly, now and always.'

She nodded. 'Good. Because I'm totally in love with you too.'

'There might be difficult days and nights ahead...'

She squeezed his hand. 'When you love someone, you face these things together. I would never walk away, Tom. I know it might not be easy but we can do it together.' Her voice was shaky with emotion and she wasn't aware she was crying until Tom gently brushed away her tears.

Very slowly and without his eyes ever leaving hers, he put his hands on her waist, drawing her in closer to him. Finally, she was able to lay her hands on his forearms, feel the muscles flex beneath her touch. She looked down at them and smiled.

'What is it?' he asked.

'I've always had a bit of thing about your arms,' she admitted.

'Yeah?' He gave a low chuckle as he tightened his arms around her and brought his lips down to meet hers. Molly slid her hands up his chest and onto his shoulders, feeling the tension in his body slowly start to yield as their kiss grew deeper.

Finally, reluctantly, they pulled apart. Tom lifted his hands to unclip her hair so that it tumbled around her shoulders and Molly felt her cheeks glow and her eyes sparkle as his eyes roamed her face.

'I'll never let you down, I'll never hurt you,' he said softly.

She looked at those beautiful blue eyes and she saw love and her future. She thought she could quite possibly stare into them forever. With a happy sigh, she took Tom's hand, leading him to the door. She opened it and turned, smiling.

'There are some people I'd like you to meet.'

# Epilogue

## Four months later

Molly wrapped her coat tightly around her as she walked to her car, feeling the biting cold of the wind. But then it was November and she was living on the east coast of Scotland.

She drove her car along the winding coastal road thinking of the lesson she had just finished. Of all things, she never would have imagined she'd be teaching golf to children. It was only a few lessons a week to young children but she loved it.

Every now and again she had to pinch herself, hardly believing how much her life had changed. The last few months had been a whirlwind in every sense and Molly didn't think it was possible for her to be any happier.

A short while later she pulled up at Willow Cottage and smiled, seeing Tom and Monty waiting for her. As she climbed out of the car, Monty wagged his tail enthusiastically, but didn't stray far from his master. Since Tom had brought the gentle Collie cross home from the rescue centre, they were practically inseparable. Tom had named him Monty, after a special dog he had met once. Monty thought he was a very lucky dog because he was rarely alone and got to spend the day with Tom at the golf school. He had also learnt to retrieve golf balls which everyone seemed delighted with.

Molly felt her heart flip as Tom put his arm around her, pulling her in for a kiss. After buying Willow Cottage, Tom had moved in a few weeks ago but today Molly was moving in.

Judy and Harry had come back from New Zealand after what by all accounts was an amazing experience for both of them and Judy had moved back into her flat while Harry had returned to his own home. Although they considered themselves a couple now, both were content to keep their own space and Molly couldn't be happier for them.

'Should I carry you over the threshold?'

'We're not married,' she laughed.

'You know I'm going to keep asking you.'

'I'm depending on it.'

Molly couldn't wait to marry Tom but didn't want to rush. She wanted to wait just a little longer, to savour simply being a couple. She followed him through the front door now and she gazed around.

'There's so much work to do,' she said happily. 'Where do you think we should start?'

'The bedroom. Definitely,' Tom said nuzzling her neck. Tom still had difficult nights but at least he was able to associate the bedroom with more pleasurable things now. Much more pleasurable.

'I was thinking the kitchen actually,' she giggled.

'Spoilsport.'

It was impossible for Molly not to cast her mind back to when she and Colin had viewed their house. Then, everything had been perfectly new and shiny with absolutely no work to do. Here, everything needed work and Molly was delighted by that. She banished thoughts of her old life – there was to be no more dwelling in the past. Her life in the city was now over. A couple of trips was all it had taken to pack it up. Apart from a few personal items and clothes, she had given everything to charity. This was a whole new start.

While Judy had been in New Zealand Molly had moved into her small flat and had happily immersed herself into her work at the inn. She had done lots of research into golfing packages available in St Andrews and had discovered a gap in the market.

She now organised specialised packages for couples, the most popular of which included a golf lesson, a round of golf and a romantic gourmet meal. Molly had also come up with the idea of converting one of the inn's downstairs storerooms into a luxury spa room so that ladies could also have treatment. In the morning guests enjoyed a leisurely breakfast served either in their room or in the dining room. She was now exploring the idea of singles golf packages.

Molly divided her time between the inn and the golf school. She spent a few days a week at the inn, managing the golf packages and helping with much of the administration, giving Judy more free time.

It had been Tom's suggestion that Molly give lessons to young children. At first, she'd dismissed the idea but he had persuaded her to give it a go and now she loved it.

Tom was working hard on his recovery and Molly was proud of him. Now he had a formal diagnosis of post-traumatic stress disorder and was seeing a counsellor, things were slowly improving. Tom had taken Molly to meet his mother and his family in the village where he had grown up. Tom's mother had been warm and welcoming, her pride for her son obvious to see not only in her face but in the cabinet she kept full of gleaming trophies.

Tom looked at Molly lovingly now. 'When is everyone arriving?' he asked her.

'Stuart and Anna are picking the kids up from school and then coming straight here.'

Molly couldn't wait for the children to see the house, especially

Lily who she was so proud of. There had been a few wobbles but she had settled into her new school and so far, things were going well. Anna was very excited about starting her bed and breakfast in the spring – and was having great fun with Eva who was designing the rooms for her. They were thinking along the lines of a French colonial style, last Molly knew.

'Did you see Joe at the school when you left?' Tom asked her. 'He was locking up and then going to collect Beth. She's doing great but I think she's looking forward to getting out before the baby is born, even if it's just to our little housewarming'

'I'd better get the champagne then. Sounds good doesn't it? Our housewarming.'

Tom grinned at her, pulling her in close. 'Sounds wonderful.' And as they waited for everyone to arrive, Molly knew she had found her forever home at last.

# Acknowledgements

Thank you to my editor, Hannah Smith, and the HQ Digital team for all their work and support on the West Sands books.
A special thank you to my family, especially Martin.

Dear Reader,

Thank you so much for taking the time to read this book – we hope you enjoyed it! If you did, we'd be so appreciative if you left a review.

Here at HQ Digital we are dedicated to publishing fiction that will keep you turning the pages into the early hours. We publish a variety of genres, from heartwarming romance, to thrilling crime and sweeping historical fiction.

To find out more about our books, enter competitions and discover exclusive content, please join our community of readers by following us at:

🐦 @HQDigitalUK

f facebook.com/HQDigitalUK

Are you a budding writer? We're also looking for authors to join the HQ Digital family! Please submit your manuscript to:

HQDigital@harpercollins.co.uk.

Hope to hear from you soon!

**If you enjoyed *Summer at West Sands Guest House*, then why
not try another feel-good romance from HQ Digital?**

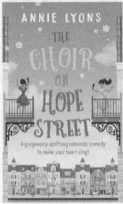

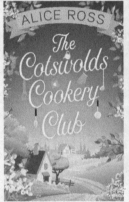